"The official announcement will be made in the morning, but I'm here to inform you, miss, that you have been elevated from afternoon-tea organizer to the position of queen of Riyaal."

The words echoed hollow in her ears. "I...*quoi*?"

She shook her head. He hadn't said that. It was impossible.

"It's very possible," he murmured, and she realized that she'd spoken those last words aloud.

Anaïs shook her head again. "You're mistaken. I can't be queen."

One corner of Javid's mouth twisted up in that irritatingly charming way. "I'm afraid it's already been decided." Was that regret in his tone?

"You're afraid? Then withdraw whatever this is supposed to be. I can't be queen," she stated again, stronger this time, as if forcing the words out with more power would erase this situation.

His head went up, his face assuming an implacable regal expression that left her in no doubt that he was royalty. "The council met a week ago. It is decided."

"Then *un*decide it!"

The harshness of her voice made him stiffen. "This isn't a raffle where another winner can be picked if the previous isn't agreeable or available. You're the only name on the list."

Brothers of the Desert

Born to rule. Ruled by temptation!

Desert royals Tahir and Javid have a lot to do if they plan to propel the kingdom of Jukarat into the world arena as a superpower. But being heirs to a powerful nation on the rise is no easy feat... Especially when passion becomes part of the equation!

Bound by duty, the brothers have always put their nation first, but the pull of the forbidden is something neither could have predicted. And soon it becomes just as important as the throne they were born to protect...

Read Tahir and Lauren's story in
Their Desert Night of Scandal

And read Javid and Anaïs's story in
His Pregnant Desert Queen

Both available now!

Maya Blake

———

HIS PREGNANT DESERT QUEEN

HARLEQUIN
PRESENTS

HARLEQUIN®
PRESENTS™

PLEASE RECYCLE
THIS PRODUCT IS RECYCLABLE

Recycling programs
for this product may
not exist in your area.

ISBN-13: 978-1-335-58405-2

His Pregnant Desert Queen

Copyright © 2022 by Maya Blake

For questions and comments about the quality of this book, please contact us at CustomerService@Harlequin.com.

Harlequin Enterprises ULC
22 Adelaide St. West, 41st Floor
Toronto, Ontario M5H 4E3, Canada
www.Harlequin.com

Printed in U.S.A.

Maya Blake's hopes of becoming a writer were born when she picked up her first romance at thirteen. Little did she know her dream would come true! Does she still pinch herself every now and then to make sure it's not a dream? Yes, she does! Feel free to pinch her, too, via Twitter, Facebook or Goodreads! Happy reading!

Books by Maya Blake

Harlequin Presents

The Commanding Italian's Challenge
The Greek's Hidden Vows
Reclaimed for His Royal Bed

Brothers of the Desert

Their Desert Night of Scandal

The Notorious Greek Billionaires

Claiming My Hidden Son
Bound by My Scandalous Pregnancy

Ghana's Most Eligible Billionaires

Bound by Her Rival's Baby
A Vow to Claim His Hidden Son

Visit the Author Profile page
at Harlequin.com for more titles.

CHAPTER ONE

JAVID AL-JUKRAT NEVER made promises he couldn't keep.

He accepted he had many and varied flaws. Hell, he *thrived* on his playboy reputation. More often than not, it fooled the unsuspecting into not taking him seriously until it was too late. But his word was his bond. And he had the clout to back it up.

It was why he excelled in diplomacy after all. Why his long-suffering brother, the ruling Sheikh of Jukrat, bit his tongue repeatedly and gave Javid the freedom to do the one thing he cherished and excelled at.

It was why Javid now dragged his head up from his three-thousand-thread-count silk pillow, cracked one bloodshot eye open and fixed it on the young, sharply dressed aide, standing at the foot of his bed, brimming with purpose and levelling a gimlet stare his way.

And delivered a new promise.

'I will triple your Christmas bonus and guarantee you an aide post anywhere in the world if you go away and let me sleep for another hour. You, more than anyone, know I can make it happen.' His voice sounded like churned gravel and felt like it, the result of too much drinking and too much enthusiastic celebration of the carnal kind.

Who could blame him?

He enjoyed female company and wasn't afraid to vocalise his appreciation of a warm, willing woman in his bed. And last night's activities had been particularly...*athletic*.

Speaking of which...

He cracked his other eye open, breathed a sigh of relief when he saw he was thankfully alone in the endless expanse of his Californian king-size bed. While he was enthusiastic about company, he was unyielding about guests staying over without his express permission. Which was rarely given.

Dragging his focus back to the undesired presence of his aide, he saw the man positively bristling and curbed a frustrated smirk. Somehow the young man had managed to locate an insult in his offer.

'Your Highness, I wouldn't be doing my job if I didn't ensure you were promptly informed of time-sensitive matters as and when they arose...'

Javid groaned, dragged a pillow over his head and happily drowned out the rest of the affronted speech. Quick on the heels of his relief that he was alone, he was wishing for the return of the

vibrant and bendy redhead who'd kept him lust-
ily occupied until the early hours.

He was absolutely certain Wilfred wouldn't
have interrupted him had she still been in his bed.
What exactly was so important that he had to
suffer the staid assistant berating him at—dragging an arm beneath the pillow, he peered at the
Vacheron Constantin watch on his right wrist, and
groaned again—*five-seventeen a.m.*?

Several minutes of blessed silence passed, but
Javid knew better than to hope Wilfred had chosen discretion over valour and vacated his bedroom. Hell, he could feel condemning eyes boring
into his naked back.

With another frustrated grunt, he tossed the
pillow away and jackknifed upright, valiantly ignoring the stilettos of pain gleefully announcing
the hangover from hell.

'Think carefully before you plot your next
move, Wilfred. Unless this matter concerns the
welfare of my brother or sister-in-law, my mother
or whatever straggles of blood relations I have remaining, you may very well find yourself unem-
ployed before the half-hour strikes.'

To his credit Wilfred recognised Javid's tone of
voice. It was the one he used when he was done
pursuing his beloved diplomacy and reached for
the big guns. Several halls of parliament and coun-
cils around the world had heard this very timbre

of voice, and those wise enough to heed its warning usually granted his wishes.

It was why his brother let him get away with murder.

It was why he'd seduced more than his fair share of female heads of states and CEOs.

'Well?' he barked, his patience ebbing.

A paler Wilfred swallowed, then again, to his credit, straightened his spine. That steely determination was the reason Javid had hired him. He never backed down no matter how much Javid barked and bit. Very few had been able to handle his moods. He'd learned it the hard way by going through six assistants in three years. So far Wilfred had lasted eighteen months.

He wouldn't last much longer though, if he continued to stand there, mute.

As if he sensed the imminent explosion, the young man lifted his head.

In the second before he spoke, a curious rush of…*something* blew over Javid's nape. He didn't believe in premonition or fate or any of that nonsense. But he did recognise regret when he saw it. Same went for apprehension.

Hesitancy. Caution. Pity?

All emotions that flashed across Wilfred's face.

He dragged a hand through his dishevelled hair, his jaw clenching as Wilfred opened his mouth. Whatever was coming wasn't going to be pleasant. At all.

'It's about Their Majesties, King Adnan and Queen Yasmin of Riyaal,' Wilfred said, the tiniest waver in his voice.

An exhale exploded out of him, something tight and heavy easing within him. The only people he truly cared about in this world were his brother and, lately, his new sister-in-law, Lauren, and his brand-new nephew. He could stretch to caring about the people of Jukrat that his brother ruled over, but only because Tahir's whole life was dedicated to caring for his subjects and, by association, Javid cared too.

Beyond that…his gut tightened as his thoughts swung to the father who'd died fully intractable in his disapproval and rejection of his second son. Who had never had a kind word or voiced encouragement for Javid. Ever.

He let loose a bitter smile.

Javid had repaid that injustice with a life of excess he knew would incense his father. And they'd been bitter and estranged long before the old man had breathed his last.

As for his remaining parent…

His smile evaporated. He knew where he stood with his mother. She didn't pretend to love him, and he didn't pretend to care. He allowed her to shamelessly use his name to advance herself in her Parisian social circles as long as he didn't have to suffer the indignity of the sham dinners and get-togethers that she demanded of Tahir.

He hadn't exchanged more than a handful of words with her in five years—most of those at his brother's recent wedding—and he was more than fine with that.

He ignored the grating discomfort in his chest and narrowed his eyes at his assistant. 'These past seven days in California have been a gift to myself after months of dealing with my cousin and the many problems plaguing his kingdom. You know this because you cleared my calendar and ensured the trip was work-free yourself, correct? And I gave you a few days off to enjoy *yourself* at a five-star hotel, remember?'

'Of course, Your Highness.'

Javid winced. No matter how many times he asked him to use his first name when they weren't in company, Wilfred refused. With grim amusement, Javid promised himself he'd remove the stick stuck up his assistant's backside before their relationship was over, if it was the last thing he did.

First things first, though… 'Then, by everything holy, why are you bothering me about Adnan and Yasmin again?' he griped.

He'd fulfilled his promise to Tahir. Hell, he'd *over*-fulfilled. The six months he'd initially agreed to spend in Riyaal managing Adnan's dire policies had turned into nine, the deplorable state of affairs a challenge few others would've risen to. Javid had walked a fine line between frustration, aggravation and diplomacy. He'd bitten his tongue so many times, he was stunned the organ still functioned.

But he'd done his duty and helped Adnan avoid several international incidents and crippling trade disputes with his neighbours and the world at large. He'd left several trusted individuals in high level positions to ensure his careless cousin's kingdom didn't end up on the brink of collapse, or, worse, of a possible *coup d'état* fuelled by his own disgruntled subjects, again.

Satisfied with a job well done, he'd hopped on his private jet to California to celebrate his success and freedom in style. And he'd got off—pun intended—to a great start.

Which left him at a loss as to why Wilfred was determined to—

'Your brother has been trying to reach you for a few hours, Your Highness. When he couldn't, he had his aide contact me at the hotel.'

Javid tensed. 'Why?'

Wilfred cleared his throat. 'King Adnan and Queen Yasmin were flying back from their summer residence when their helicopter went down. The wreckage was discovered in the early hours of yesterday morning. Your Highness… I'm sorry to report, there were no survivors,' Wilfred said, his voice solemn.

The curious breeze blew again. Harder. Turning Javid's whole body ice-cold. The hand in the process of raking through his hair dropped to his side, his insides sinking before turning numb.

As much as his cousin had been an obstinate and reckless fool with very little knowledge of practical rule, he'd been his blood. And Yasmin... had been pregnant with their first child.

Sorrow and regret churned through him, his uncharitable thoughts of moments ago flaying him open with shame.

Rising from the bed, he strode to the floor-to-ceiling window overlooking Santa Barbara's multimillion-dollar view, his jaw clenched tight. He now understood why his aide had disrupted his sleep. Tahir had wanted to break the news to him before Javid discovered it through unsavoury channels.

'His Majesty still wishes to speak to you,' Wilfred reminded him.

Javid exhaled again, a keen suspicion that his vacation was about to be cut woefully short whizzing through him. Tahir would want him at the funeral, of course. Perhaps even seek his advice as to who would be best placed to take up the mantle his young cousin had tragically and far too soon vacated.

Even as he turned from the window and headed across the master suite into his sumptuous bathroom, he was conducting a shortlist. Many would jump at the chance at the throne, but Javid knew only a handful would truly be up to the task without getting drunk on power and falling into the same pitfalls his late cousin had almost succumbed to.

'Inform my brother I'll be ready to speak to him in fifteen minutes. And organise the appropriate statements and wreaths to be delivered to the palace.'

'Yes, Your Highness.' Wilfred was already on the move, his strides purposeful.

Fifteen minutes later, Javid was dressed in a sombre, bespoke dark suit, his pristine white shirt neatly tucked into his trousers and dark tie in place. He'd shaved his week-long stubble and his hair was neatly combed, his fingers steepled before him as he waited in his private study for the digital connection to his brother.

In record time, the playboy prince was neatly tucked away, and the diplomat had re-emerged. Others had likened that switch to a chameleon. Javid liked to think it was clear-minded, uncompromising willpower. He knew what he wanted, when he wanted, and he made no apology nor had reservations about achieving his goals.

Tahir's face flickered onto the screen and Javid held his breath, his gaze searching his brother's, that curious knot still tied in his chest.

He knew why he searched.

They'd never had happy childhoods, he and Tahir. As the heir to the throne, his brother had had it much worse, he knew. In some deep dark place he didn't like to explore, Javid suspected his shameless descent into excess had been his own way of taking the spotlight off his brother.

As a newly married, ostensibly happily, man, Tahir had displayed all the signs of marital bliss with the woman who'd markedly blighted his life for a long time. While he was willing to wish his brother every happiness, Javid couldn't seem to find it in himself to truly believe Tahir was happy. Hence the need to search beneath Tahir's steely gaze, to assess whether his purported bliss was real or the more familiar pseudo-affection he was used to from his mother. From the women who trailed through his life without ever being allowed to touch him because he knew they were after one thing only—a chance to bask in the spotlight of his royalty, his wealth, his sexual prowess, his brilliant mind.

His brother's gaze narrowed, as if he was sensing and disapproving of Javid's thoughts. Javid regretted the flash of anger that lit Tahir's eyes before his brother neutralised his expression, knowing that questioning Tahir's happiness would be considered a deep slur.

For a second, Javid lowered his own gaze, and when he raised it, he'd neutralised his own, his focus on the grave news that had necessitated this meeting.

'We're sure they both perished?' he asked, his voice low.

Tahir's nostrils flared as he inhaled audibly. Then he nodded abruptly. 'It's been confirmed. The official statement will be released later this morning, but the news cycles are already picking it up.' The barest grimace clenched his features until control reasserted itself.

Allowing himself another bite of regret for the young lives lost, Javid leaned forward. 'I'll clear my schedule to attend the funeral. I'm drawing up a list of candidates to act as interim rulers until an official council forms to...' His words trailed away when another peculiar look crossed his brother's face.

'The council has already been formed.' Javid worked out the time zones and nodded as his brother continued. 'We met first thing this morning. You would've been part of it if you'd been available.'

Just like with Wilfred, Javid felt the eerie sensation dance over his skin. But seeing as this was from the ruler of a formidable kingdom and the man who bore the same warrior blood that surged through Javid's veins, the look was far more potent. Enough to tie several knots in his gut. Enough to capture and strangle the breath in his lungs.

'Well, I'm available now,' he said tightly, resenting the mild rebuke. He'd done his diplomatic duty, and he'd happily walked away.

Yes, it grated that he'd missed the council meeting, but, in the long run, didn't it mean one less thing for him to do?

He'd craved freedom ever since he'd recognised that being around his parents meant having front-row seats to rejection and recrimination. Excelling in his studies in diplomacy had been the perfect avenue to serve his royal duties while removing himself from his father's presence. At a mere twenty-one, he'd left Jukrat and rarely went back.

He'd made homes in California, Cairo, the South Pacific, and half a dozen more destinations around the world. With a private jet and unlimited funds at his disposal, he'd carved out a specifically 'solitary unless company was needed' life for himself. One he didn't intend to change or apologise for.

So what if waking up next to a different woman with cringing frequency was beginning to lose its pall? It was just a passing phase. His appetite was plenty healthy enough to withstand the odd fallow period. He simply needed to revisit old stomping grounds or discover new ones. *Or both.* Hell, perhaps it was time to buy the new mega-yacht he'd been promising himself and leave *terra firma* for the open seas with a blonde or three in tow.

He gritted his teeth as his brother leaned back, his dark gold eyes boring into him. Seeing far too much. 'Are you?'

The hairs at the back of his neck stood up. Again, he ignored it. 'If you didn't call to request my help in forming the new council, then why did you call?'

'Because certain decisions have been made that you need to be aware of.'

A flash of ire whipped through him. 'If my input wasn't necessary, why do I need to know after the fact?'

The barest hint of a smile tugged at Tahir's lips. 'I didn't say it wasn't necessary. On the contrary, it's vital now.'

'Stop dancing around the issue, brother. If you don't need me, I have several meetings I need to be getting on with.'

The smile evaporated and he held his breath again as his brother leaned forward. 'I need you, Javid. Perhaps now more than ever. Because *you* were the only candidate in contention.'

'Candidate in contention for what?' His voice was razor-sharp and he didn't apologise for it. Because that premonition he didn't believe in? It was burrowing its way through the conversation, positioning itself in the centre of his consciousness in a way that hugely unsettled him. 'Actually, no. Do not confirm what I think you mean, brother,' he warned, a heaviness shaking through his voice that drew even weightier contemplation from his brother.

'It's impossible for me not to.'

Six words. Six earth-shaking words.

'You know Adnan had no other close blood relations besides us. And I'm out of the running, for obvious reasons. Which means—'

'No!' Javid jerked to his feet, pivoting from the wide screen as if placing distance between him and his brother would halt the inevitable juggernaut heading his way. 'Not today. Not tomorrow. *Never!*'

Tahir's face hardened. 'It's already been decided.'

Javid whirled around, baring his teeth in what he knew was a mirthless smile. 'You know better than to pull that stunt with me, brother. Remember who you're talking to. Nothing is ever definitively decided, especially when one party actively resists.'

Tahir gave a brisk nod. 'I remember who I'm talking to. You're the ultimate rebel with the Midas touch. You scandalise with one hand and perform diplomatic miracles with the other...when you wish to. Is that the threat here? That you'll destroy everything you've helped build in Riyaal just to prove a point?'

'I'm saying you should've known better than to present me with what you think is a done deal,' he said through gritted teeth. 'Especially one you know I don't want. Ruling was *your* destiny, not mine.'

His brother's face twisted but his expression wasn't as hard or as embittered as it'd been once upon a time. For a single moment, Javid wondered if that was Lauren's doing. Then he shook the thought free. Whether it was or not didn't matter. His immediate goal was disentangling himself from the ropes his brother was attempting to bind him with.

'You're wrong.'

'Excuse me?' he breathed, basking in the fresh anger that whipped through him. Anger he understood. Frustration, too, was a familiar bedfellow. What he didn't relish was this foreboding that kept dogging him. As if this conversation was already a foregone conclusion. That whatever he said or did, it would only end up one way.

'You walk into a room and change opinions. You leave a room and lives around the world change for the better. You fool yourself into thinking you're removed from your actions but everything you do alters destinies. Tell me, brother, what is that if not a form of rule?'

Javid felt his jaw sag before he brusquely took control of himself. 'Don't be absurd.'

Tahir didn't respond, merely returned his livid stare with a steady one of his own.

'I have four perfectly good candidates for interim rule,' Javid snapped, then reeled off the names he'd collated even before he'd taken his shower.

Tahir nodded. 'All brilliantly positioned to form part of your council of advisors.'

Javid pinched the bridge of his nose, the hangover initially blazing at his temples now turned into a pounding pain throughout his whole body. 'You're not listening,' he growled.

'I'm listening, brother. To the instinct that tells me no one but you is best suited for this. You resolved the trade deal and steered Riyaal from an impending free-falling economy in a matter of months. You're better skilled than all the candidates put together.'

'But you're wilfully overlooking one thing—I. Don't. Want. The. Job.'

Tahir's eyes hardened, and in that moment Javid saw their father. Sure, his brother's eyes didn't contain the permanent censure and contempt his father's had held, but a shiver lanced down his spine all the same. It was enough to hold his tongue, to lock his knees as Tahir leaned forward.

'But you're blood, Javid. And Riyaal needs you. After fighting so hard to help Adnan's people, are you truly going to let them down now?'

It was a low blow. But in many respects, Javid respected his brother for his ruthlessness. It was a trait they shared; one *he* wasn't above exploiting when it suited him. He would've been more disappointed if Tahir had tried to cajole him.

Of course, his fury intensified as he watched his brother nod to someone off screen. And when a knock came at Javid's study door and Wilfred walked in, he didn't need to open the leather-bound folder placed in front of him to know what it contained.

When his aide activated another screen that showed one of the very men Javid had intended to handpick for the interim ruler position, he felt the claws of inevitability sink deeper into him.

Eyes narrowed, he glared at his brother. 'What is he doing here?'

'Your aide and soon-to-be chief of staff are bearing witness so they can get the relevant balls rolling.'

'You may think this is a foregone conclusion, but I have demands of my own. Several, in fact,' he grated out.

Tahir's lips twisted. 'Read the document. You'll find I've anticipated a few of them.'

Javid turned his attention to the document in front of him, his gaze darting over the words crafted to seal his fate as ruler of a kingdom he didn't want.

Halfway through, his gaze flew to his brother's. 'Fifteen *years*? You want me to commit to fifteen years before another ruler is even considered? You're joking, right?'

'How long do you propose?'

'Five,' he snapped, already thinking he was being more than generous.

'Twelve,' Tahir countered.

'No. I'll give you seven. That's more than enough.'

'Ten. You of all people know how long it takes to entrench good, lasting governance.'

Javid clenched his jaw. Ten years was usually his own recommendation during diplomatic negotiations. Talk about being hoist by his own petard. 'Fine. Ten. Not a second longer.'

Tahir smiled and Javid knew he'd been played like a Jukrati fiddle. Fighting his temper, he returned to reading. Only to choke on his shock on the next page. 'A *bride*? You expect me to marry, and you've already picked a bride for me?' he snarled in disbelief.

Tahir was no longer smiling. But there was a flash of sympathy in his eyes when he answered. 'Unfortunately, brother, the council deemed that part non-negotiable. As much as I don't agree with it, it's been decided. The day before your coronation in three weeks' time, you'll marry the late Queen's cousin.'

CHAPTER TWO

ANAÏS DUPONT HAD reached the stage of grief where anger freely flooded her veins. She'd gone through the shock and denial. Sobbed into her pillow at night when depression struck and bargained futilely with the fates while watching her beloved cousin's body being lowered into her grave alongside her husband.

Now she was fully ensconced in anger for the senseless death of her beloved cousin. For the baby she'd never get to meet.

But most of all, she was angry at the news Riyaal's palace councillors had delivered to her yesterday morning, three short days after the funeral.

The dispassionate and indifferent way her intention to return home to France had been curtailed. *As per a request from the leader of the high council.* Whose identity was wrapped in mystery.

And then the stomach-hollowing news that, far from the quiet departure she'd expected, she was to be given a new role altogether.

One to be divulged *in due course.* As if she

had nothing better to do than sit around, twiddling her thumbs.

But wasn't that what she'd done for the better part of three years as her cousin's lady-in-waiting? Yasmin, rest her soul, had been nothing more than a figurehead queen, an ornament on her husband's arm, brought out and displayed when the occasion called for it, and then placed back on her superluxurious shelf, whiling away her time organising exquisite afternoon teas and gossiping with her friends and courtiers.

To be fair, her cousin had been content with that; and utterly blissful when she'd fallen pregnant. For that, Anaïs couldn't fault her.

But in her dark, shameful moments, hadn't she wished she'd stayed in France and written a letter or email instead of travelling to Riyaal to offer her personal condolences to her cousin when Yasmin's mother had died?

Hadn't she used her cousin as an excuse to alter the sense of her own life slipping away, and reconnected with the woman she only remembered vaguely but fondly as a child in Aix-en-Provence?

In the months after her arrival, hadn't she wished she'd taken a little more time to consider the position before jumping at the chance to live in another country?

Of course, it had been a different story recently, just before Yasmin's death. For one thing, her

cousin had quickly become the queen of a kingdom at the brink of turmoil.

Suddenly, Anaïs's days weren't spent gossiping
over petits fours and coffee but in soothing her
newly pregnant cousin's nerves as she alternated
between morning sickness and worrying about
her husband and the unrest unravelling through
Riyaal.

Anaïs might have abandoned her profession as
a PR executive in France but even she'd known
that Yasmin's husband, King Adnan, was slowly
sliding into a PR disaster that would prove detrimental to his rule sooner rather than later.

So she'd been relieved at the announcement of
an independent advisor. A renowned diplomat
Adnan had baulked against for all of five minutes before he'd embraced the offer from Sheikh
Tahir Al-Jukrat of Jukrat.

Anaïs had breathed a sigh of relief. Until, at
what turned out to be the first of only a handful
of meetings, everything Anaïs had heard about
the playboy-prince-turned-diplomat had been confirmed.

She'd watched him effortlessly charm every
woman in sight at his welcoming state dinner,
his rugged features, shameless arrogance and that
deadly smile ensuring every female in the vicin-
ity gravitated to him like iron filings to a magnet.

Except her…of course.

She'd steered clear of Javid Al-Jukrat that night

and in the months following. Had welcomed the realisation that he would spend most of his days cloistered with King Adnan discussing matters of state, and fulfilling the task he'd been sent to perform.

What he did at night was of very little concern to her. And if she'd found herself wondering how the drop-dead gorgeous pillar of masculine magnificence was spending the hours between dusk and dawn, wondering who the hapless female gracing his bed was—of which rumours had been rife—well, she'd given herself a stern, effective talking-to and gone about her own duties.

Because once bitten and all that.

Bitterness twisted her lips.

Playboys such as the scandalous prince were the reason Anaïs had been happy to leave France behind for a spell. It was why she'd accepted the job of doing next to nothing, a chance to lick her wounds in a desert kingdom thousands of miles away from her homeland, after what Pierre had done to her.

All because she'd deigned to believe she could change a leopard's spots by the sheer power of her devotion. With her intelligence and wit, instead of the voluptuous curves, overt sexuality and breathless, vacuous adoration it turned out her fiancé preferred despite his many claims that Anaïs was the one for him.

Sensible, pragmatic Anaïs.

Boring Anaïs.

She shook off the recollection of their last confrontation and resumed pacing the suite, eyeing the double doors to her suite as irritation flared anew.

She'd been kept waiting for almost two hours already. The flight she'd hoped to catch had long left. The car she had been gifted by Yasmin and Adnan still sat in the garage. Anaïs knew she could leave if she truly wanted, the high council be damned. But loyalty to her cousin kept her in check. That, and the need to ensure she wasn't upsetting any protocols Yasmin and Adnan had valued. Perhaps she could, deep down, profess to curiosity about this new role being hinted about.

Anger receded for a moment to be replaced by anxiety. She didn't pay much mind to palace gossip, but Anaïs was aware of the rumours surrounding her cousin's and the King's deaths. Rumours that the helicopter's failure hadn't been the random, unfortunate accident it'd been ruled as.

She shook her head, unwilling to indulge in dangerous thoughts.

Javid Al-Jukrat's advisory tenure in Riyaal had dissolved the mounting tensions. While his personal reputation might be extremely scandalous, his professional proficiency was impeccable. His leadership was what the council heads of states vied for with fervent enthusiasm. Why, despite his primary allegiance being to his fatherland of Jukrat, he commanded absolute kings' ransoms with his diplomatic services.

Under other circumstances she would've even admired—

No.

She couldn't admire such a man. An indiscriminate Lothario who left shattered emotions in his wake whether knowingly or unknowingly. And Anaïs could never accommodate such an individual because they, without fault, were irrepressible monsters incapable of reform.

Mon Dieu, why on earth was she thinking about him consistently?

Whirling about, she started for the farthest part of her living area when she heard the firm knock.

Crossing the room once more, she yanked the door open, ready to vent her ire.

'It's about time I was told what's going—' She stopped, her jaw sagging when the very person she'd been thinking about materialised before her.

He filled her doorway, which was something considering her suite boasted double doors that soared almost ceiling high. The Jukrat prince brought his own force field with him, a force that expanded as the silence ticked between them, as her gaze rose up and up to collide with bright eyes that rivalled the desert sun at sunset.

Eyes that held her captive as she pondered the various shades of colour that swirled within the depths. It wasn't gold or tawny like his brother's. There were flecks of bronze that seemed to ripple and flash, commanding the recipient of his stare to keep looking into those eyes she was sure had the power to hypnotise without him so much as lifting a finger.

'Otherwise you will what, Miss Dupont?'

The mocking tone dragged her back down to earth. Her gaze dropped, releasing her, thankfully, from those mesmerising eyes. But the next destination was no better.

Because his attention-grabbing lips twitched with sardonic amusement. She had noticed that about him at their first meeting.

Javid Al-Jukrat liked to treat women like playthings. Those who didn't fall into his bed were treated with mildly amused contempt; dismissed as being beneath his regard.

Anaïs told herself she'd kept her distance because she hadn't wished to engage with him on any level, but she would've had to be dead from the neck down not to notice the effect he had on everyone else.

Sensing the power and authority bristling from him, she was reminded again why she'd kept him at arm's length.

This close, his masculine scent trailed into her nostrils, the ruggedness of his jaw drawing attention once more to his face. Unlike most of the upper echelons of royalty, he didn't favour traditional clothes. Bespoke suits emphasised his flawless physique. From midnight-dark hair to the tips of his polished Italian shoes, he reeked with the sort of self-assurance that set her teeth on edge.

It took a moment to register that her jaw was clenched tight, her fists balled.

He took all of that in, one eyebrow slowly elevating as his amusement deepened. 'Are going to answer me? Or are you going to do me bodily harm?'

Behind him, she spotted a dozen guards spread along the hallway and frowned. 'What are they doing here?'

'Invite me in,' he commanded.

'Why would I want to do that? You've obviously taken the wrong turn. This is my private suite.'

'I am well aware of that, Miss Dupont.'

She stopped her shock from showing on her face as his response tunnelled through her. Then she attempted to look over his shoulder. 'I'm waiting for whoever called this meeting to arrive and explain themselves to me. I have places to be.'

All trace of amusement left his face. 'And where would those places be?'

She glanced down at her watch just for a little relief from the force of his presence. 'Back home to France, if you must know. The plane I was supposed to catch left an hour ago. I don't intend to miss the next one.'

'That won't be happening,' he said with that same sardonic gravity that settled heavily into her.

'What's that supposed to mean?'

He stepped forward, forcing her to take a step back. She blinked in shock after he turned and shut the door behind him.

'I don't recall inviting you in.'

'Then I hope you will apologise for the discourtesy eventually.'

'Excuse me?'

He strode past her, making a beeline for the spacious living room that adjoined her bedroom.

Seething, she followed him, unable to drag her gaze from the rugged shoulders and the streamlined body that strode with animalistic ease into her personal space.

She watched him cross to the imposing ornate mantel at the far side of the room. And found herself holding her breath as he swivelled to face her.

'Sit down, Miss Dupont.'

Rebellion darted through her and she opened her mouth to retort. But at the last moment she held her tongue. Whatever Javid Al-Jukrat was here to discuss, it was nothing personal. It couldn't be.

He'd dismissed her at their first meeting as inconsequential and she'd returned the favour in the months that had followed. When their paths had crossed, they had been chillingly cordial. But she was aware the council had met since the funeral, and she sensed Javid might hold the information she hadn't been able to access thus far.

Even if he didn't, he was royalty. As much as his presence jarred her, she couldn't exactly throw him out.

Striding to the seat farthest away from him, she perched on it, and folded her hands in her lap. Tilting her chin up, she raised an eyebrow.

He observed her movements again with a trace of amusement, but it eventually dwindled away and she was faced with the imposing pillar of masculinity she couldn't, for the life of her, resist staring at.

'We buried your cousin only a few days ago. What's the hurry to leave?'

Shock mingled with the darts of pain as she stared at him. 'I didn't realise my activities were any of your business. Or that my mourning was to be conducted in a certain way that suited you.'

One shoulder lifted in a shrug that again commanded her attention. *Mon Dieu*, she really needed to stop being aware of his every little movement.

For the first time she saw a muscle twitch in his jaw that said that he wasn't as relaxed as he wanted to project. 'According to palace records, your position here was as a lady-in-waiting and confidante to your cousin, correct?'

'Why do I get the feeling you already know the answer to that?' she countered.

'I'm just puzzled as to why you're in a hurry to

leave. Is there another position of doing next to nothing waiting somewhere for you?'

Anaïs told herself the heat in her cheeks was from anger, not embarrassment. He had no right to look down his nose at her in that contemptuous way.

Did he?

'Did you come here just to insult me, Your Highness?' She injected as much chill into her voice as she could summon.

Again, one corner of his mouth twitched but this time there was no amusement in sight. 'You've been part of the royal household long enough to know that appearances mean everything.'

'And what does your appearance here mean exactly?'

For a moment his gaze settled in the middle distance. Was he giving thought to what he was about to say or…was he unwilling to say it? But then his gaze sharpened, his eyes turning a burnished gold that once again mesmerised her.

Dragging her gaze from his face, she looked down at her lap for a moment before settling it somewhere at a point between his shoulder and neck.

'For clarity's sake, I'm the one who requested the meeting,' he stated.

She swallowed, unease weaving through her. '*Bien.* For what purpose?' She hated that her voice

wavered a little, that whatever he was about to say
felt like a monumental event.

'You were the Queen's confidante, which I'm
assuming means you're able to maintain some discretion?'

Her bristling intensified and she shot to her feet.
'I'm not sure why you feel the need to issue veiled
insults. Is this how you treat women who don't fall
over themselves at your feet?'

His eyes widened a touch, and, to her eternal
irritation, his lips moved again in hard amusement, dragging her gaze once more to the line of
the lower lip that seemed a little too full. A little
too sensual for a man. She fiercely resented that it
immediately evoked thoughts of what she could do
with those lips, even while she was unable to stop
heat from flaring through her system, pooling low
in her pelvis and reminding her that, though she
hadn't sought male attention for a while, she was
still very much a red-blooded woman.

A *virgin*, true, but a woman, nevertheless.

'I'm merely trying to establish your purpose
in the palace.'

'Of course, you are. And I'm the Virgin Mary.'

This time both eyebrows shot up, and his chest
moved in a way that made her realise, stunningly,
that he was chuckling. 'That's…interesting.'

'No, it's not,' she exclaimed hotly, annoyed with
herself for the telling train of thought. More than
a little flustered, she waved a hand at him. 'Let's

get this over with, please. And before you say anything, I've never felt the urge to join in palace gossip groups.'

He nodded. 'Good. It's in your best interest not to.'

'Again, why?'

'Because your next role is going to be a little bit more challenging than sitting around discussing Paris Fashion Week and drinking tea.'

'I'll save you the trouble, Your Highness,' she said immediately, the need to be done with this making the words trip out. 'I don't want a new role. My bags are packed and I'm leaving here this afternoon—'

'Bags can be unpacked,' he stated. As if she was an idiot.

Anaïs took a deep breath, hoping it would clear her head and dispel the eerie sensation that felt as if she was no longer in control of her life. He advanced towards her.

It was a slow, languid stroll, as if he either had all the time in the world or was unwilling to spook her. But with each stride, she felt the calm she was feverishly willing into her body evaporating. When he stopped a few feet from her, sliding his hands into his pockets, her throat moved in another convulsive swallow.

Mon Dieu, but he was something else. Something far too detrimental to her peace of mind.

'The official announcement will be made in

the morning, but I'm here to inform you that you have been elevated from afternoon-tea organiser to the position of Queen of Riyaal.'

The words echoed hollow in her ears, bouncing around until they thudded hard in shock. 'I… *quoi*?'

For a moment, she wished she hadn't surged upright. True, she'd barely eaten since her cousin's death, and grief had a way of messing with one's head, but surely she hadn't heard him say…

She shook her head. He hadn't said that. It was impossible.

'It's very possible,' he murmured, and she realised that she'd spoken those last words aloud.

Anaïs shook her head again. 'You're mistaken. I can't be Queen.'

One corner of his mouth twisted up in that irritating charming way. 'I'm afraid it's already been decided.' Was that regret in his tone?

'You're afraid? Then withdraw whatever this is supposed to be. I can't be Queen,' she stated again, stronger this time, as if forcing the words out with more power would erase them.

His head went up, his face assuming an implacable regal expression that left her in no doubt that he was royalty. Javid Al-Jukrat might have spent most of his adult years in the Western world, but he was very much forged from the blood and sinew of Arab warriors. 'The council met a week ago. It is decided.'

'Then *un*decide it!'

The harshness of her voice made him stiffen, and all traces of humour left his face. 'You seem to think you have a choice in the matter.'

There was a certain level of cynicism in his voice that drew her gaze to his face. Also present was a sliver of resignation. Before she could decipher it, he was speaking again. 'This isn't a raffle where another winner can be picked if the previous isn't agreeable or available. You're the only name on the list.'

More than the veiled insults again, his words struck even more alarm through her. Alarm she forcefully discarded. Because this was ridiculous.

And she had a plane to catch.

Turning away, she headed for her bedroom, ignoring her shaky legs as she snatched up her handbag, then turned around only to freeze with a gasp as he strode into the room after her. As she grappled with the sight of a man...*this* man...in her room, his gaze went from her face to her handbag and back again.

'You still seem to think you're going somewhere,' he drawled.

'That's the benefit of living in the twenty-first century, Your Highness. I'm free to do as I please. Tell the council to find someone else to be their queen. I'm not interested in the job.'

For some reason those words activated a grim smile. 'There seems to be a lot of that going around. But unfortunately for you and me, it doesn't mean anything.' The gravity of his words shook through her.

Her fingers tightened around the straps of her handbag. 'That's absurd.'

'It's not,' he stated with graver finality.

Dragging every last shred of her composure together, she strode towards him.

He remained still; his hands firmly wedged in his pockets.

'I would appreciate it if you would get the hell out of my way, Your Highness.'

The fractional widening of his eyes told her she'd surprised him.

Why that triggered a frisson of excitement through her, she chose not to examine.

'At the very least, this process won't be boring,' he mused with another hard edge to his tone.

She paused within a few feet of him, a different thought occurring to her. 'Why are you here to deliver the news instead of the council members? I know Adnan was your cousin but…'

'But what?' he prompted a little tersely.

'The funeral is over. Shouldn't you be returning to wherever it was you came from?'

His nostrils flared, as if she'd broached a touchy subject. 'My presence is very much needed here. Essential, some might say.'

That eerie feeling returned, harder than before. She felt the bones in her hands protest and looked down to see that her fingers had tightened even further on bag straps.

'If the council has chosen the Queen then they must have chosen the King too?' Something tingled through her, her heart beating faster as she stared into his face.

He didn't answer, just continued to hold her gaze with eyes that flashed with emotions she couldn't quite name.

'Your Highness?'

'Javid,' he murmured, his tone low, deep, with a rumble that corkscrewed through her in places she didn't want to name. 'When we're alone, you may call me Javid.'

More sensations unfurled, flitting through her belly and delivering sparks between her legs. 'Why would you and I ever be alone together?'

'Because, as you've surmised, the council have chosen the new ruler of Riyaal.'

She felt the blood drain from her head, far too many sensations bombarding her as she read the truth she didn't want to know in his face.

'Let me spare you the suspense, shall I? In ten days, I will ascend to the throne of Riyaal and assume the mantle of its new King. Shortly after that, you, Miss Dupont, will take yours as my queen.'

Javid told himself not to be insulted by the rush of rejection that followed hard on the heels of her shock. Rejection that stayed as she shook her head, her lips working, and backed away from him.

'*Non.*'

He gritted his teeth, disturbed and supremely irritated by her reaction. It was that same dismissiveness she'd shown him the first time they'd met several months ago when he'd arrived in Riyaal.

They'd barely been introduced before she looked through him as if he didn't exist, then spent the whole of the state banquet ignoring his presence. He was used to women pretending not to notice him, a ploy designed to give an air of exclusiveness that barely withstood the course of a meal, never mind the entire evening.

Not Anaïs Dupont, though.

She'd maintained the frosty attitude at their few meetings, treating him like a nuisance she couldn't wait to be rid of.

It was only because his duties to Adnan had been so all-encompassing that he'd shoved her attitude to the back of his mind. The situation that'd greeted him on his arrival in Riyaal months ago had been such that there had been no room for dealing with Anaïs Dupont.

But there was no ignoring it now.

She'd not only rejected the position of Queen outright, but she was also distressed at the thought of marrying him.

As he watched her a different sensation wove through him. The tiniest thrill at the challenge she posed. It was one he hadn't encountered in a while. He relished the word rolling off his tongue as he answered, 'Yes.'

Her eyes widened, and Javid felt as if he were being absorbed into the turquoise depths. Were they real?

He shook the thought away, growing more annoyed with himself.

The senior members of his newly formed council had offered to deliver the news. An offer he'd immediately rejected, much to his own chagrin.

The challenge. Yes, that was it.

For some reason, this woman posed a challenge he couldn't resist. Perhaps on another level, he'd wanted to relay the news face to face. The way he preferred. He was a diplomat. He knew when a situation called for soft negotiations.

Except he didn't feel soft around her.

Her rejection and resistance continued to grate. But that pale flawless skin he wanted to stroke made blood pool in his groin. Made his senses stir as they hadn't in a long time.

'Queens are chosen from blood relatives. You're familiar with that, aren't you?'

Her head moved in a jerky nod, the careless knot she'd tied her silky hair into at risk of failing. He'd never seen her with her hair down in all his time in Riyaal, he mused absently. And then he fought against the need to stroke his fingers through the mass, explore the silky lustre of her hair.

What the hell was wrong with him?

He'd thought he'd sated himself well with the blondes and redheads in California. This whole situation was getting to him. Hell, he should be back in California, enjoying his freedom.

Teeth gritting harder, he continued, 'Then you'll know, as Yasmin's only living relative, that makes you the only choice according to Riyaal law.'

He watched, unnerved as she squeezed her eyes shut, as if willing him away. Almost of their own volition, his feet ushered him closer, until her floral scent hit his nostrils.

He sucked in a slow deliberate breath, drawing her scent further into him. He was sure he'd absolutely hate it once he had his fill of it. He preferred fruity scents to flowery fragrances on his women.

Yet, the faint scent of what he guessed were lilacs was intriguing. Alluring enough to make him want to take another breath. And another.

'Surely there must be some other way,' she said, her voice imploring.

He frowned. 'Why do you act as if this is a prison sentence?'

She blinked, her eyes slowly filling with that irritation that made them sparkle. 'You may have jumped at the chance to wear your dead cousin's crown, but I'm not in a hurry to take a position I think someone else would be better suited to.'

Javid froze, the combination of anger and grief knocking together to produce a growl in his throat. He caught himself just in time, telling himself his time was better spent not rising to her bait. As surprisingly stimulating as it was.

'You think you won't be suited? All those years of doing nothing?'

'I wasn't doing nothing. I was offering the support that was needed.'

He allowed his lips to curl, enjoyed seeing how that irritated her. 'Then you have nothing to worry about. If you prefer you can carry on doing exactly nothing when you're Queen. All I ask is that you take an interest in your people every now and then.'

A tremor shook through her. Her breathing grew agitated, enough to drag his gaze down to her chest, to the fullness of her breasts and the alluring cleavage displayed by her sundress.

The punch of hunger to his gut surprised him. Clearly his celebrations in California hadn't quite scratched his itch.

He watched as her fair head deliberately tilted, her gaze growing distant and mocking. 'I didn't think you were deaf, Your Highness. There will be no marriage. I will not be your queen. Find someone else.'

'Ah. A challenge. I'm not sure what I relish more—a reluctant queen or her eventual capitulation.'

He watched heat flow into her cheeks, her eyes sparking even further. Before she could speak, he raised his hand and, as was tiresomely familiar, she fell silent at the command. 'You signed documents when you were absorbed into the royal household. Part of those documents included your agreement to any position the ruler of the house required you to take. This ruler has chosen you as his queen. There is no escaping it.'

He turned, and then paused to glance over his shoulder. 'I suggest you get used to the situation quickly. News of our wedding will be announced tomorrow. Our marriage ceremony will take place before the month ends. And if for nothing else, for the sake of Yasmin and everything she held dear, you will show up for it.'

CHAPTER THREE

SHE WAS GOING to be Queen.

For two long weeks she'd tried to wrap her mind around her new reality. While she hadn't exactly been looking forward to returning to France, it had been a normal she knew.

Looking around her now, nothing was normal. She'd been well and truly flung into the unknown.

She was going to be Queen.

Despite her every resistance.

For three days straight, she'd argued and cajoled and all but threatened the council to change their minds. Javid had countered her every argument. With that perpetual trace of mocking amusement that continually drew her attention to those sensual lips.

But in those days too, Javid's last statement had resonated and continued to grow in her consciousness.

For the sake of Yasmin and everything she held dear...

Even while she'd advocated for someone else,

someone infinitely more qualified, her conscience had prodded her. Was she letting Yasmin down by her vehement refusal? What if whoever else they found was even worse than she feared she would be?

As the days had gone by, the weight of those words had grown too heavy to shift. That, and the council's refusal to even consider anyone else because Anaïs had signed her name to an agreement that propelled her into the role, had eroded vital layers of her resistance.

While she was still scrambling for a solution, this was a role she'd have to get used to very quickly because the relentless preparations for her wedding were well under way. For the last week, designers had flown in from Paris, Milan and New York to consult with the Riyaali retinue of planners she'd been assigned.

In another week, an elaborate ceremony would take place and her role would be official. A fact that still made her reel in shock.

She rose from her seat in the sitting room of her new quarters. She'd drawn a line at inhabiting her late cousin's suites. While she couldn't avoid the destiny marching towards her, she at least had a say in where she slept within the palace. Unfortunately for her, the only available rooms besides the late Queen's had been in the west wing, along the hall from where Javid slept, with interconnecting doors to boot.

Apparently, one sheikh several rules past had installed those chambers so he could have access to his mistresses.

She'd dismissed any significance of that aspect from her mind. Just as she'd done while Javid had been on his diplomatic mission, she intended to keep her distance from him. The clinical way this marriage had been arranged suited her perfectly. It would be a marriage of convenience for the stability of the kingdom. Just as Javid had said. Whether she slept in the suite next to his should matter very little.

Striding across the sitting room, she stepped out onto the large terrace and breathed in the cool mid-afternoon air, hoping it would calm her nerves. But the only thing that arrived was increased anxiety.

The announcement of Javid as the newly elected ruler of Riyaal had been met with surprisingly rousing acceptance by the majority of the population. Hell, an early poll had shown that he was significantly more popular than his cousin had been, whereas her new role had been met with scepticism. It was scepticism that continued to churn through her stomach. Yasmin might have been a little removed from her connection with her people, but she had nevertheless been beloved.

What if she, Anaïs, drove her new subjects to misery?

'My Lady, I'm sorry to impose, but we really

need to get on with choosing the paper for the card placement settings.'

Anaïs gritted her teeth, the pressure at her temples pounding harder. The last thing she wanted to do was pick out which embossed paper went with which colour of napkin for her wedding. But she'd learned very quickly that no one made a move without her full endorsement.

She didn't want or need that sort of power. And yet here she was.

She took a deep breath and turned. The trio of women awaiting her next instruction stared back at her with a mixture of apprehension and pity. And for a moment, she wanted to scream with the futile energy bubbling inside her. But she forced her fists to loosen, her chin to lift, and took another breath.

As much as she'd hated the reiteration from Javid, she owed it to Yasmin to do her best for her cousin's beloved kingdom.

So, for however long she remained in the role, she would.

Tabling that *however long* discussion with Javid for later, she summoned a smile.

'We'll go with the dark cream and the midnight-blue lettering. Instruct the archivists that we will use the eighteenth-century cutlery set for the coronation banquet.'

Anaïs watched them spring into action, guilt and apprehension keeping her a little bit removed from the whole thing. She was thankful that her years-long experience as a trouble-shooter for her old PR firm had kicked in. And for the next few hours, she powered through her seemingly endless to-do list.

But just as she was beginning to crave reprieve, Faiza, the woman who'd been assigned as her private secretary and aide, the role Anaïs herself had occupied only a handful of weeks ago, looked up with a smile.

'The last thing on your schedule this afternoon is tea with His Highness.'

Her gaze shot up, that irritating sprig of excitement blooming beneath the skin. 'I don't recall that being in my diary today.'

Faiza's smile dimmed a little, traces of anxiety flashing across her face. 'Oh, I hope you don't mind, but His Highness's aide requested an hour in your schedule, and I thought, since it was likely we'd be done by now, that…' She shook her head. 'I can cancel if you want me to?' she enquired hesitantly.

Anaïs shook her head. She had questions she wanted to clarify with him anyway, so perhaps this was a good chance. 'It's fine. I'll go to the tea.'

She knew she'd made the right decision when relief replaced the panic on Faiza's face. She might be rabidly averse to being in Javid's presence but there was no advantage in announcing it to the world and alienating those who yearned for a little bit of joy to replace the recent tragedy.

Fifteen minutes later, she was blessedly alone.

Entering the dressing room that was easily three times the size of the studio apartment where she'd lived in Paris, she stopped to examine herself in the full-length mirror.

The Chanel suit she'd worn for her meeting with the wedding planner was still fresh and suitable for her meeting with Javid. Raising her hand, she touched the chignon at the back of the head. Satisfied that it would also stay put for the next few hours, she opened the glass cabinets that held a stunning array of make-up and accessories.

Just like the suit and every other item of clothing in the dressing room, it'd come courtesy of her new role.

Selecting a tube of pale pink gloss, she ran it over her lips, ignoring the slight tremble in her hand. It wasn't because of Javid, she assured herself. It was because every decision she made regarding this role had to be taken carefully. The last thing she wanted was to cause more upset in the kingdom.

And yet, that fizzle only intensified as her heels clicked along the marble floors leading to Javid's office.

As had happened increasingly over the last week, as news of her role had taken hold in the palace, everyone she met offered a deferential salute.

Anaïs wished she could go back to the time when she'd been all but ignored whenever she was at Yasmin's side, then immediately regretted the thought. If she could go back, she'd first wish for her cousin to still be alive.

She breathed through the punch of grief that lingered, taking another breath that went nowhere to sustain her lungs as the imposing doors leading to Javid's official domain came into view.

A middle-aged man she knew had been Adnan's senior aide approached. 'His Highness is finishing a call. If you would like to come in and wait?'

She nodded, and, with a dry mouth and jumping nerves, followed him into the inner sanctum.

As had happened far too often in their recent interactions, her gaze darted across the room, seeking out the man behind the antique oak desk of the royal office.

And as had also occurred in those moments, his gaze was waiting for hers, that quietly ferocious expression she'd come to associate with Javid Al-Jukrat, fixed on her.

She vaguely took note that he was speaking fluent Mandarin, and that the aide who had shown her in had quietly retreated. But she was vividly aware that she'd frozen in the middle of the office, the eerily hypnotic effect of his gaze having stopped her in her tracks.

Mon Dieu, but everything about this man was ferociously riveting.

More and more, she was beginning to recognise what it was about him that had women losing their minds. It was the way he moved; the way he watched a woman with single-minded focus—as if, in that moment, she were the only person that existed. Not that she intended to fall prey to that disease.

She had learnt her lesson thoroughly and unforgettably with Pierre.

The reminder effectively unfroze her, even as he jerked his chin at the sitting area of his palatial office. The silent instruction sent heat crawling over her cheeks, and she turned away with less grace than she desired, but welcoming the chance to remove herself from his open scrutiny.

It was only then that she spotted the staff member standing discreetly next to the polished silver trolley that held a varied array of sandwiches and finger food together with pots of tea and coffee.

Anaïs chose a single stuffed armchair, that almost animalistic need to always put the distance between Javid and herself dictating her actions.

Arranging her hands in her lap, she crossed her ankles and straightened her spine.

'Would My Lady prefer tea or coffee?'

She tried not to huff at the term. If she thought

this was burdensome, in a handful of days it would change to a much weightier address. One that she quietly panicked about when she dwelled on it too much.

She summoned a smile. 'I'll take tea with milk, no sugar. *Shukran.*'

With another shallow bow, the staff member strode away to fetch her beverage while, from across the room, she heard Javid finish his call.

Studiously avoiding looking his way, she accepted the tea and a plate of sandwiches when the attendant returned, set them down next to her, then kept her gaze on her teacup as Javid murmured in Arabic to the young attendant. While she understood and spoke a few words, her grasp of Arabic was below rudimentary. And even as the strong smell of his coffee reached her nostrils, she deliberately postponed the inevitable clash of their gazes until she heard the servant retreat.

Eyes the colour of copper coins were waiting for her, pinning her to her seat. 'Ah, there you are. I was beginning to wonder whether you were going to ignore me for the duration of our meeting.'

'A feat you would've made impossible, I'm sure.' Her voice emerged much primmer than she'd intended but she inwardly shrugged it away. She would never be at ease with this man, and she had no problem with that. Hell, the warier she was of him, the better she could keep her wits about her.

'How well you already know me,' he said, the low rumble of his voice intensifying within her. 'I would've achieved very little in life if I allowed such things to stop me. Have something to eat,' he encouraged before she could respond, nudging the plate of food towards her.

She'd taken numerous breaks throughout the day and the usual impeccable palace meal service had been readily available to her. But the knots in her stomach had prevented her from taking full advantage.

As if he were personally responsible for it, a rumble echoed in her stomach, triggering another flush in her cheeks.

What was it about Javid that made her as gauche as a schoolgirl? Irritated by his effect on her, she shook her head. 'The tea is enough, thank you. And if you don't mind, I'd like to get on with why I'm here.'

For a tight stretch of time that breached the boundaries of politeness, his gaze rested on her. Then he took a leisurely sip of his espresso before setting the saucer on his knee.

Anaïs couldn't help her gaze from dropping to the delicate china held in his big, capable hands. There was something…visceral about that display of caged strength that drew heat into her pelvis.

Which was such an absurd thought, she was almost relieved when he spoke.

'I thought it would be prudent to catch up. Everything going well with the wedding arrangements?' he asked. Everything about him seemed indolent. Languid. Except for the laser sharpness in his eyes. Those missed nothing. She would be wise to bear that in mind.

She opened her mouth to give him a perfunctory response. Then paused. Women were far too quick to say everything was fine when they didn't mean it. She'd been bashing her head against the wall, but she wasn't quite ready to miss the opportunity to give it one last shot. 'I worked in PR. I can spot a disaster when I see one. I still think it's not too late to cut your losses.'

All traces of humour evaporated from his face. 'With that sort of defeatist attitude, maybe I should.'

Annoyance bristled her skin. 'I'm not defeatist. I'm being pragmatic.'

'Obviously you've been out of the PR game for too long. Wouldn't you be trying to find a solution instead of throwing in the towel before the challenge has even begun? Is that what you'd tell a potential client? That they should give up without even facing whatever challenge had been thrown at them?'

She shook her head. 'This is much bigger than that.'

'It's not really. Every problem, big or small, has a solution. Name one thing that you think is insurmountable,' he said.

'Yasmin was pregnant when she…' She rallied through her sadness and pain. 'The kingdom was overjoyed by the news. How are you going to deal with that expectation when the people start making noises about an heir to the throne?'

His face closed up so tightly, she feared his jaw would shatter. She should congratulate herself. Clearly, she'd found the one subject the great Javid Al-Jukrat couldn't mock or bat away. For the longest time, she thought he wouldn't answer. And when he did, his voice was ice cool, clipped. 'Children are not part of my immediate future plans, and I expect not in yours either. So we will have to placate the Riyaali people some other way.'

She shouldn't have felt that sharp loss of breath at his answer. Shouldn't have imagined for a fleeting second that his answer would be different. Just because his brother, the Sheikh of Jukrat, treasured his newborn son it didn't mean Javid would be tripping over himself to father children. And even if he did, in what world did she imagine it would be with her? When this was to be a *sexless* marriage of convenience?

'I'm still awaiting an answer, Anaïs. Do you have what it takes to fight, or will you throw in the towel before the crown is on your head?'

He was as obstinate as a blind donkey. *'Dieu aide moi,'* she mumbled under her breath.

One eyebrow quirked in amusement. 'Invoking the aid of a higher power so soon? Shouldn't you wait for the first week after our wedding, at the very least?'

He spoke French. Of course. 'Is everything a joke to you?'

A flash of bitterness shattered his amusement. 'Far from it. But that is not to say I don't take my pleasures where I can.' The lazy fire of his gaze trailing her body imprisoned her speech for several seconds. And before she could summon a rapier-sharp put down, he was speaking again. 'Speaking of pleasures…'

'Pardonne moi?'

A different sort of flash lit his eyes then, as if her words had elicited something dark and delicious. Something…carnal. That he didn't bother to hide it made her squirm in her seat. Anaïs tried to breathe through the sensation, to ground herself in the more important reason she was here.

'I have no wish to discuss any sort of *pleasure* with you.'

'You spit that out like it's a bad word, *habibti.*'

Anaïs had heard that word often enough during her time in Riyaal to know what it meant. And to know he was toying with her further by calling her darling.

'Your Highness—'

'Javid,' he insisted, the narrow-eyed, laser-like precision in the look he sent her telling her that he would be obeyed in that.

'Fine. Javid.' She stopped, took a breath.

For some reason, uttering his name caused tiny flames to ripple down her neck, and flare all over her body like an upside-down blush. What on earth was wrong with her? She'd never felt this way around Pierre. And *he'd* been the man she'd intended to spend the rest of her life with.

Oui, and also the man who'd let her down in the most humiliating, spectacular fashion. The reminder threw cold water on the flames and, while she didn't welcome the memory, it calmed her long enough to formulate her thoughts. 'I have several things to be getting on with, so I'd appreciate it if we concentrated on more important subjects.'

'And you deem the subject of pleasure unimportant?'

'Why does it matter?' she asked with more exasperation.

'We are about to get married. You don't think I have a right to know the state of your private sexual life?' he returned tightly, with a quirk of his eyebrow.

In the grand scheme of things, it was a pertinent, if aggravating question. 'And would you be answering *my* questions on the subject or is this a one-sided thing?'

Lounging back further in his seat, he waved a regal hand at her, and, while his amused look didn't return, the ferocity in his eyes didn't abate. 'You have a moderate window to ask me anything you require. It's only fair since I will be requiring the same openness from you.'

She had expected a sexist answer along the lines of him being a man and therefore not requiring the same accountability, not for his acquiescence to satisfy her curiosity. But now that she'd been given the green light, Anaïs found herself reluctant to ask. For some peculiar reason, she didn't want to know the ins and outs of Javid's sex life. So she shrugged. 'I think the tabloids keep enough of a running tally of your exploits for me to know the true state of them.'

'You disappoint me. Don't you want to hear the truth straight from the horse's mouth?'

His response brought to mind a wild Arabian thoroughbred; the kind people paid fortunes for. The arrogant King of the stables who knew they were a prized possession and let everyone around know it too. The kind with the thoroughly potent virility—

'Now, that look on your face is interesting. I'm eager to know what you're thinking about me,' he rasped, a thicker note to his voice that shot that blazing arrow straight to her pelvis again.

'You're assuming I have any interest in you at all,' she managed haughtily.

His face hardened and, for a fraction of a second, she saw his hand tighten on his tie before he relaxed once more. 'Be that as it may, any previous sexual liaisons on my part will cease with immediate effect, naturally. I expect you to give me your assurance that the same goes for you?'

Anaïs wanted to laugh, then blurt out the shocking truth that, not only did she not have a lover, but she'd also never slept with anyone in her life.

At the last moment, she counselled herself out of it. At the very least he would be shocked, as some were when she divulged that bit of information. Or at the most, she would invite another bout of searing mockery.

She couldn't really abide that today. Certainly not from a man as sophisticated and utterly assured in his sexual desires as Javid was.

'Answer me, Anaïs.'

She jumped, aware that this was one of the few times he had addressed her by name. The first time she'd heard his perfect French intonation of her given name. And heaven help her if that didn't send a resurgence of that illicit thrill through her.

Huffing out a breath, she answered, 'There is no lover or significant other.'

She saw then that he hadn't been as relaxed as he'd projected. Because at her response, he set his coffee cup down and truly sprawled on the sofa, his eyes gleaming with light that could only be termed triumphant. 'Good. Very good.'

'Now that we've got that out of the way, can we discuss how long this…enterprise is supposed to last for?'

His eyebrows clamped in the dark frown. 'Excuse me?' His tone was Arctic frost.

'Rulers come and go, whether they be kings or queens. I may have agreed to this marriage for now, but I don't think any law in any land can keep me in this position indefinitely. So I ask again, when can I expect my freedom?'

Considering his own position and reaction when Tahir had informed him of his new role as King of Riyaal, Javid was unnerved by the depth of his strong negative reaction to her question. Yes, there was a stench of double standard to it, but he'd never claimed to be perfect.

The fact that she too wanted to be free should have bounced off him.

And yet the thought of Anaïs walking away, perhaps even sooner than *he'd* agreed to, sent a wave of disquieting rebellious rage through him. That it came hard on the heels of the other curious sensation that had spiralled through him, one of intense satisfaction that there was no lover lurking in the background, served to darken his mood.

The problem couldn't possibly be…*him*…could it? He shifted in his seat, disquiet growing into true disconcertion. He must be losing his touch if handling one prickly female was causing him this much discomfort.

The tug of challenge had him leaning forward. 'Don't you think you're jumping the gun a bit? You could realise, in only a matter of weeks, how much you enjoy being Queen. Don't you want to wait a while before clamouring for freedom?'

She sent him a look that suggested she had his number. But she didn't. No one did. He played his cards too close to the chest for that to be a flaw.

'You don't go into negotiations blind. Why do you expect me to do the same?' she asked.

'I may not go in blind, but I do have a level of faith.'

Her eyes widened. She hadn't expected such an answer from him. Javid hid a smile. Most people expected him to toss out rigid and practical solutions. But he'd learned long ago to be flexible to achieve his aims.

'Does that surprise you? That I rely on faith?'

Her long, lush lashes swept down, confirming his suspicion, and for a moment he revelled in her discomfiture, revelled in the tinge of colour that swept up her cheeks. And then she was raising that pointed, sexy little chin that drew his attention to her heart-shaped face. Those plump lips that pursed far too often for his liking and begged to be softened with a kiss.

His kiss.

He shifted again as she answered. 'I'm afraid faith falls low on my priority list.'

'What comes first?' he asked, curious despite himself.

'In my experience, a man who has honour and integrity. Who makes a promise and sticks to it.'

The vehemence behind her words threw another log of curiosity into the fire blazing within him. He watched her, unable to take his eyes away from the challenge she posed.

'Then let me make you one that will set your mind at rest. Commit to fully to being my queen and you won't have cause to seek your freedom.'

Husky laughter spilled from her lips and had it not been a grave subject, he would've laughed with her.

'Something funny?'

Elegant shoulders shrugged. 'I find it amusing that you seem to think that I only need to jump through the hoops that you set for me in order for me to find fulfilment. Isn't that just like a man?'

'Are you labelling me sexist?'

'If the shoe fits,' she said.

Javid was mildly offended. He had been called many things, but sexist hadn't been one of them. Until now. He paused to examine her words. He had delved into enough situations to know that her answer stemmed from a definitive source. And he had enough baggage of his own to recognise the shroud covering hers. He continued to watch her and, after a few minutes, she began to fidget.

'We established that I'm not going to take your words on faith. So, where do we go from here? Personally I would like to commit a specific time frame. Maybe two years?'

He tilted his head, the urge to delve beneath her words clawing harder into him. 'What are you so afraid of?'

Her eyes widened again, her gaze staying on his for several seconds before it shifted again. Those lips that looked pillow soft even from across the room pursed again. 'Why do you keep trying to make this something it isn't? Did it occur to you that I'm doing exactly what you suggested and putting the interests of the people first?'

Enlightenment spiralled to the surface. 'You don't think you're good enough?' The words were barely a murmur, surprise making them hushed.

In all their interactions, he'd been presented with a self-assured woman, one who didn't mince her words or prevaricate to suit the situation the way he was used to with the women in his private life.

But there she was, stunning the hell out of him again. And not in a good way this time. Eyes narrowed, he struck to the heart of the matter. 'Who made you think that you weren't good enough?' he demanded.

Her guarded expression dropped and for several seconds she merely stared at him, shock in her eyes. Then her expression shuttered, blocking him out effectively. 'It's…no one. I don't have the first idea why you'd assume something like that.'

Javid chose to let her rushed denial go, forcibly suppressing the curiosity that clawed at him. 'Then prove me wrong.'

She opened her mouth, ready, he was sure, to argue with him further. But he raised his hand, effectively silencing her.

'I'm open to discussing this further on down the road but there will be no time frame.'

He shrugged away the voice taunting him for his hypocrisy. After all, if she lasted as long as he intended his own rule to last, then they could go their separate ways with no hard feelings. And if it occurred before then…his jaw gritted, that bite of rejection at the idea striking him again.

He was attempting to digest those sensations when she rose. And as had been occurring on a frequent basis, his gaze dropped down her body, cataloguing every attractive feature. And there were many.

Granted, she wasn't his usual type; he preferred women with more curves. But he couldn't dismiss the fact that her body flared and dipped in all the right places. As for that insufferable attitude, he'd come across it often enough in his professional life to know that a woman who challenged him cerebrally was a woman who would also entice him into her bed. Not that he planned on anything happening between them.

The taunting voice whispered again but he ignored it.

'I see we're not going to agree on this. For now, I will let it be but, make no mistake, I won't hesitate to pick up the matter again and act on it if I feel the need to. You forget that, as the queen you're so eager for me to become, I'll have powers of my own to do the right thing.'

Meaning if she felt that she was letting the people of Riyaal down. There was something obscurely admirable in there somewhere, but he wasn't going to reveal his feelings at the moment. Instead, he nodded. 'You have my word that we will discuss it if the need arises.'

An expression flitted across her face, and on anyone else Javid would have deciphered it as gratitude. But it was gone almost instantaneously and that expression of derisive dismissal was slotted firmly in place.

Perhaps it was that infernal need to win, a characteristic that had been cultivated in him when all he had done was lose as a child, that ignited to life inside him. But even before he had taken his next breath, he knew he was going to take pleasure in wiping that look off her face.

Anaïs did not know it, but she had just started a battle between them that he knew he would win.

'Are we done here?'

He allowed a smile to tilt his lips. 'We are far from done, *ma petite*. Frankly, we're only just beginning.'

He watched her absorb the words, different expressions flitting across her face.

Whether it was the endearment he'd used or the gravity behind his words, he didn't waste time considering. Instead, almost against his will, his gaze travelled over her again, his fingers itching to flick open that resilient button holding her suit jacket closed.

He wanted to explore the neat trimness of her waist, to trace his fingers over those cheeks again to confirm that they were as soft as he remembered. But he forced himself to remain seated. There was no point in spooking her before she was his queen.

There would be time enough to explore this curious need to tangle with her whenever she was within touching distance.

'But yes, that'll be all for now,' he dismissed, keeping his voice low. 'You may go.'

At that, she lifted her chin, no doubt taking offence at that too. But just then, the phone on his desk began to ring and the weight of the role he had barely taken on pressed down on his shoulders. He didn't cross over to answer it immediately, rising and crossing over to her as she smoothed her hands over her skirt.

Catching his gaze on her, she immediately

stopped the action and turned away, her movement so regal, he wondered whether she knew she was already projecting the role she was about to undertake.

A role that he was beginning to think had more interesting challenges in the form of his future wife than he had originally anticipated.

'Anaïs.'

She steeled herself against the decadent shivers that trickled through her at the sound of her name on his lips.

'*Oui?*' she murmured, then grimaced inwardly once more. She really needed to stop reverting to French. The only times she'd done it around him was when she was flustered. And they both knew it.

'We have my coronation rehearsal tomorrow and our wedding rehearsal a few days after that. I expect to see you at both.' They were words to further imprint on her that this union was happening.

What are you so afraid of?

Two years ago, she would've said 'nothing'. But circumstances had eroded a few vital layers of her confidence. As much as she was loath to admit it, it was why she'd left France; had jumped on her cousin's invitation to visit.

Are you going to hide for ever?

The voice that sounded far too much like her late mother's straightened her spine. For Yasmin's sake, she'd do her duty as best she could, for as long as she could. But she still reserved the right to change Javid's mind as to her suitability. 'I will be there,' she answered primly.

And then, pivoting on her heel, she walked straight out of his office, her head held high.

CHAPTER FOUR

ANAÏS DISCOVERED JUST how adept Javid was at *managing* her in the days that followed.

Every request she made for a meeting was deftly and politely batted away, every joint event—and they were numerous and piled with enough heavy *protocol* to make her want to tear her hair out—filled with a dozen or more people vying for his attention to make stating her case further infuriatingly impossible.

Not even at his coronation, a jaw-dropping ceremony that drew awe and global fanfare and guests from around the world, was she able to find a few minutes alone with him. Instead, she watched from several feet away, the new, heavy and elaborate diamond and platinum engagement ring delivered to her suite that morning weighing on her finger as a crown was placed on his head. As that head rose proudly and he intoned his solemn commitment to the throne and to his rule over his increasingly adoring subjects.

Javid knew about her futile attempts, and, oh, did he relish it.

He didn't miss the chance to lob a mocking smile at her over yet another state banquet table or quirk that silky eyebrow every time she opened her mouth and was instantly interrupted by some dignitary who simply needed to speak to His Majesty urgently.

As a last, desperate resort the evening before her wedding, she'd picked up her mobile phone to call him, only to realise she didn't have his number. Too embarrassed to request it from Faiza, Anaïs instead instructed her to get His Majesty on the line, only to be reminded—even though she'd had no inkling of it in the first place—that Riyaali tradition dictated no form of contact between betrothed couples the day before their wedding ceremony.

Anaïs suspected that little tradition had been made up by a man for this very reason. She'd retired to bed on the last night of her single life caught up in far too many turbulent emotions to name and in the unshakeable knowledge that, come tomorrow, her life would be inextricably linked with Javid Al-Jukrat's.

Morning arrived far too quickly. Heart in her mouth, Anaïs watched Faiza approach with a breakfast tray, a huge smile plastered on her face.

If one thing had gone right since her fate was

set, however, it was the rapport she'd struck with her invaluable assistant.

'Good morning, Your Highness.'

She sat up and buried her face in her hands. 'Faiza, I'm not sure how many times I've asked you to call me Anaïs.'

'And I've told you, Your Highness, that it's protocol written in stone,' she protested with a laugh.

Anaïs raised her head and speared her with a narrow-eyed look. 'Jot this down on your notebook. It's one of the first protocols I'm going to change.'

Faiza's smile turned speculative. 'Does that mean you're looking forward to your wedding now, Your Highness?' she asked softly.

Anaïs bit back a frustrated groan, then breathed it out, a part of her unsurprised that her astute assistant had picked up on her reticence. Staring down at the sterling silver tray that held tableware so delicate and priceless she was almost too afraid to use it, she swallowed. 'I will do what is expected of me,' she replied, her breath catching when something fundamental knotted inside her. *For Yasmin's sake.*

'That's all the people will expect, Your Highness. Especially at this difficult time,' Faiza said, her tone solemn.

That solemnity lingered for another few seconds, then Faiza stepped forward and poured Anaïs's coffee. 'The stylist and her entourage are waiting. Impatiently. I thought you might need a few minutes to yourself. But I'm afraid I won't be able to hold them at bay for much longer.'

And thus began the longest day of her life.

With both her Riyaali mother and French father gone and the distant French relatives not close enough to have been included in her immediate wedding party, Anaïs tried to keep the loneliness at bay as attendants flitted around her, primping and teasing and buttoning her to within an inch of her life.

She barely recognised herself when she rose for her long train to be positioned.

In the mirror she saw a tall, slim figure draped in the softest pale amber gown dotted with precious gemstones along the boat-shaped neckline and along the sleeves.

Sapphires, rubies, amethysts and a larger yellow diamond in the centre of the collar. That yellow diamond was replicated in the centrepiece stone on the tiara that sat on her head and in the platinum setting of her engagement ring.

Anaïs had been hesitant about wearing jewellery that belonged to her cousin, and she'd been relieved to discover this set hadn't been one of them. Her assumption that they'd been liberated from the crown jewellery vault hadn't been confirmed but at least she didn't have another weighted reminder that she was stepping into her beloved cousin's shoes.

She glanced down at her hands, the delicate henna patterns still vibrant against her skin.

The more traditional ceremony would take place tonight, but the henna had needed to be applied so it could set in time for the event.

The one thing she and Javid had agreed on—via their wedding coordinators—was to go both Western and traditional with the ceremony. Riyaal was diverse in its religious views, so Anaïs had been pleased at the chance to honour both traditions.

Another breath shivered through her as the double doors to her suite opened.

'It's time, Your Highness,' Faiza said softly.

One last look in the giant gilt-edged mirror showed a woman who looked outwardly composed, probably even serene. Anaïs prayed that illusion would hold as she turned away, the jewel-encrusted heeled slippers matching her dress barely making a noise as she glided out of her suite.

Dozens of palace staff had lined the corridors to see her. She plastered a smile on her face, thankful for the veil shielding her as she emerged into the sunshine.

The stretch limousine was purring at the foot of the palace steps.

Inside, she was surprised to see a stunning woman dressed in a beautiful emerald gown that did wonders for her bottle-green eyes and gorgeous face.

She leaned forward and smiled as Anaïs hesitated at the doors. 'I know this isn't strictly protocol but when Tahir told me you didn't have a maid of honour, I volunteered myself as tribute. Just for the ride to the cathedral. I hope you don't mind?'

'I…' She paused when she realised she was talking to Lauren Al-Jukrat, the wife of Tahir Al-Jukrat, ruler of Jukrat and mother of their recently born son, and Javid's sister-in-law. 'I don't mind but…are you sure?'

Her smile was compassionate. 'I have a fair idea what it feels like to be removed from close family at a time like this. At the very least, I can fill your ears with mindless chatter, so you don't concentrate on the butterflies in your stomach.'

Anaïs's smile this time didn't feel so tight but, if anything, the butterflies had increased. Lauren Al-Jukrat had only been Queen for a short while, but it'd taken very little time to have her subjects falling under her spell. The impact she'd made in her United Nations envoy role alone had made positive headlines around the world. Not to mention she was half of the kind of power couples *Time* magazine raved about.

'Somehow I don't think you'd be capable of mindless chatter if you tried, Your Majesty,' she said once Faiza and the stylists had helped settle her into the limo and the vehicle was pulling away on the smooth ride to the cathedral where the ceremony was being held.

'Oh, please, it's Lauren. And you flatter me, but I think my six-month-old son would beg to differ,' she said, the love and fondness in her voice unmistakable.

'Where is the young Prince?' Anaïs asked.

'With his father and the nanny. And take it from me, one of those two will be counting the minutes until I return to play mummy and wife,' she grumbled good-humouredly.

The thick vein of love and adoration in her voice made something catch inside Anaïs. While she wasn't one to lend any credence to tabloid speculation, even she hadn't missed the naked devotion Lauren and her husband felt for each other. Rumour was that they'd been involved years ago at university and had rediscovered deeper feelings for each other again recently. Lauren Al-Jukrat didn't need the light, cleverly applied make-up. She positively glowed with love when she talked about her husband and son.

Anaïs kicked herself for the jealousy that nipped at her. It was no one's fault but hers that she'd ignored the flashing signs that said leopards didn't change their spots. That Pierre's claims of being the reformed playboy was a load of nonsense. She'd been light-headed at the fact that she'd changed him. She… Anaïs, the risk-averse virgin who hadn't even had a proper kiss until she was twenty-one? Whose stumbling confession to Pierre, when he'd expressed frustration at her waiting till her wedding night, had brought a glint to his eye she now recognised as a gauntlet he'd intended to pick up and claim at all costs?

How arrogant of her to believe she'd succeeded where her own mother had failed to tame any of the no-good bastards she'd dated and attempted to change?

'Anaïs? We're here.'

She startled at the gentle prompt. Looked up and saw that they'd pulled up to the front of the cathedral. Well, at least Lauren had been right. She'd managed to take her mind off the nerves eating her alive at what awaited her behind the imposing walls of the Riyaali royal cathedral.

Except now she was here, now she was within minutes of facing her future husband, the butterflies had turned into eagles, soaring and swooping and making her nauseous.

'It'll be fine, I promise,' Lauren said, laying a soothing hand on Anaïs's knee.

From behind the veil, she sucked in a long breath and nodded.

She was being silly. She'd set out her intentions often enough over the past few weeks to know what awaited her as wife and Queen.

Except… Javid hadn't given her the chance to spell *one* thing out.

Sex.

Specifically, how he intended to proceed. It was

all well and good dissolving his past liaisons, but they'd never talked about his future ones.

And how the very thought made her—

'Anaïs?'

She roused herself and moved purposefully towards the open door. She was half French. She knew, and sometimes applauded, the power play behind being fashionably late.

Today, however, wasn't such a day. And her dawdling would only fray her own nerves.

She stepped out, then gasped softly when the deafening cheer drew her gaze to the throng crowded into the picturesque square opposite. *Mon Dieu*, surely, they weren't…

'See? They love you already,' Lauren murmured from beside her.

She shook her head. 'Everyone loves a royal wedding. I'm just the latest shiny object for them to post on their social media.'

'I don't think so, but I'll let you come to the realisation yourself. Good luck, my dear,' Lauren said before her hand found Anaïs's and pressed comfort into it. Before she could reply, Lauren glided away, a stunning figure shadowed by bodyguards she hadn't even noticed until now, leaving her alone with the expanse of the red carpet flanked by a Riyaali military in full regalia to guide her into the cathedral.

Trumpets sounded from high above her on the rooftops.

Another cheer went out in the crowd.

You can do this. For Yasmin's sake. For the kindness she showed you when you were at your lowest. Keep her people happy, even if only for a while...

Anaïs gathered every scrap of composure and put one foot in front of the other. Her grasp grew tighter and tighter around the stem of the breathtaking bouquet of purple vanda orchids and amber-coloured roses matching her dress, her heart hammering faster when she saw the thousands crowded into the vast space, their avid gazes fully trained on her.

That heart leapt into her throat one minute later when she spotted Javid.

As the new commander-in-chief of the Riyaali army, he'd chosen their deep purple military regalia and combined it with his own medals, won during his brief, mandatory stint in the Jukrati army.

For the first time since they'd met, he wasn't indolent or laconic or even faintly amused. He stood straight and proud, one hand on the scabbard propped into his belt, the other curled into a loose fist at his side. His hair gleamed under the cathedral lights, his clean-shaven face drawing attention to every chiselled angle and the sensual curve of his uncharacteristically serious mouth.

His eyes were fixed with predatory stillness on her, a fierce intensity in the depths snatching what remained of her breath.

In short, Javid Al-Jukrat, newly crowned King of Riyaal, who protocol had dictated be renamed Javid bin Jukrat Al-Riyaal, looked every inch a modern warrior king, tall, proud, and it was more than a little terrifying to be his entire focus.

Thankfully, she managed not to stumble as she completed the final steps to where he stood, his hand imperiously held out.

Someone relieved her of her bouquet and, aware of the eyes fixed on her, she slid her right hand into his. Then felt the shower of sparks that lit her from the inside out. Despite their meetings, state banquets and brief appearances together, this was the first time Javid had initiated sustained contact with her.

As much as she wanted to attribute the stomach-dipping reaction to the butterflies in her stomach, she knew it was down to the man and not the circumstances. And perhaps it was avoidance of this very reaction that had made her less than eager to touch him.

She subtly wriggled her fingers, anxious to dislodge his hold.

He held on, his gaze piercing through her veil. Then he went one better, and raised her knuckles to his lips, eliciting a ripple of murmurs through the crowd. She probed his expression, wanting to see if he'd returned to his amused mockery and was teasing her for the sake of their audience.

But no.

His expression was even more ferocious, a light shining in his eyes as his gaze moved down her body, taking in every inch of her ensemble. It lingered on the tiara for a few nerve-stretching seconds before finding her eyes.

On any other man, Anaïs would've read the look she caught in his eyes as searing possessiveness. The kind that bellowed to the world that this soon-to-be queen belonged to this king.

But they had an agreement…didn't they? A marriage of convenience didn't leave room for possessiveness or stake-claiming or the kind of look that held dark, intense promises she had no interest in making him keep.

Promises that mildly terrified her, if she was honest with herself. Because these were the kinds of intense emotions her mother had revelled in, had actively sought to elicit in her partners, turning herself inside out to drag interest from her boyfriends, which had inevitably fizzled out within weeks, leaving her out in the cold and sliding fast into another depression.

That overly recycled sequence of her mother's life had made Anaïs vow never to fall prey to her emotions. Never give the time of day to a Lothario, never mind handing over the reins of her emotional well-being to him.

Hell, hadn't she moved halfway around the world to put distance between herself and the ex-fiancé she'd believed had changed but had in essence just hidden his true colours well?

She swallowed as Javid tightened his grip ever so slightly. To get her attention. To steep her in the present.

When she wriggled her fingers this time, he released her. And as they pivoted to face the cardinal, Anaïs reiterated to herself that nothing *would* change. Her heart had sustained repeated little cuts every time her mother had forsaken Anaïs in favour of her next great love story. It'd been dealt a harder blow by her ex-fiancé.

This time, her heart would remain safe and piously protected behind the fortress she'd built for it. And no amount of sparks or fireworks would endanger it.

Balance still shaky but within sight of being restored, Anaïs intoned her vows.

Then the time she insisted she didn't dread arrived. She was officially Anaïs Jukrat Al-Riyaal. And her new, formidable husband was about to lift her veil and deliver the official wedding kiss.

Every wisp of oxygen left her lungs, the effort to believe that she wouldn't be affected straining her every nerve.

'Relax, *ma petite*, I don't intend to ravish you to within an inch of your life in front of our guests. You're quite safe.'

The words were pitched for her ears only, the tiniest trace of mockery back in his voice. But, if anything, his expression was even more intense, the lack of a barrier between them thickening the charge connecting them.

The tiniest quiver of sound broke free from her lips when his hands dropped to cup her shoulders. Already a little light-headed from lack of air, Anaïs compounded her troubles by lowering her gaze to the mouth drawing inexorably closer.

Mon Dieu, was there another man on earth with lips more sinful than Javid's? Lips that promised the wickedest heaven?

She received an inkling of the answer—that there was most likely not—a scant moment later, when those lips whispered over hers. Once. Twice.

Then on the third caress, he…lingered, fusing their lips together. Turning sparks into flames, static shivers into pure electricity that forked through her with lustful glee. Her fingers twitched and convulsed. Then she was grasping his arms, fuzzily excusing herself for touching him because she needed to do so for the sake of their audience, when the truth was she couldn't stop herself from doing so. Couldn't prevent another betraying sound from leaving her throat when the tip of his tongue swept over the seam of her lips.

Then, as her fingers dug into his flawless coat to steady herself, he ended the kiss and withdrew.

For several moments, the applause from the guests sounded like noise from under water. Then it broke through her haze, dropping her back down to earth.

Her arm was wound through Javid's, his smile suave with masculine pride as he accepted the accolades. After a moment, he bent his head to hers, his lips a hair's breadth from her earlobe. 'That rabbit-caught-in-the-headlights look you're wearing is great, but perhaps attempt a smile so our guests don't think you've been dragged kicking and screaming to the altar?'

Anaïs blinked, mild shock weaving through her when she realised they were already halfway down the aisle. Phones had been forbidden in the church, but official media outlets were recording every moment for posterity.

So, as unnerved as she felt, Anaïs summoned yet another smile, her poise barely holding as they walked out.

Again Javid paused, gently cupped her nape and brushed a shorter kiss over her lips to the roar of the crowd and of acclamatory bells pealing from the cathedral tower.

Her senses still caught in freefall, Anaïs prayed for silence as they were ushered into another sleek limo and were driven away.

But Javid had other ideas.

'You look quite breathtaking, *chère femme*. Now I understand why veils are necessary. They're to keep simple men from making utter fools of themselves before they make their vows.'

Practised words. Delivered at the right pitch in the right timbre to make a woman lose her mind. Anaïs hated herself for her inability to stop the heat spiralling through her.

Still, she summoned a cool, mocking smile of her own. 'Did you just call yourself simple, Your Majesty?'

The smile he delivered then lit pure, white-hot flames to her pelvis. 'Once upon a time, I wished that were so but alas...'

'You discovered you were far too special to ever be anything as mundane as simple?' she tagged on when his voice deliberately trailed off.

If she'd hoped to dent his thick armour of arrogance, she was to be disappointed. 'Indeed. But that is not to say your appearance hasn't struck a certain note.'

The breath she'd only just caught threatened to flee again because for some reason he'd retained his hold on her in the car and now lifted her hand to brush his lips across her knuckles once more.

Anaïs clenched her hand and reclaimed it. 'You don't need to do that. We don't have an audience.'

A trace of humour left his eyes and they turned hard. 'That's where you're wrong. There are always eyes watching. Forget that at your peril, dear wife.'

Words that proved all too true over the next few hours as their elaborate and extensive reception progressed.

As she changed from western to Riyaali attire, a breathtaking concoction of deep champagne traditional bridal gown with more complementing jewellery to match the tiara she kept on her head. With her new attire, the henna was vibrantly evident, and her attendants gasped with delight as she made her way back to the vast second ballroom, which had been decked out to host this version of the wedding.

Drums and finger cymbals heralded her arrival, and she entered the room to find a dozen male drummers lined up one side of the processional royal-blue carpet and an equal number of women rhythmically clicking the cymbals on the other. But, as seemed to be occurring terrifyingly frequently, it was Javid's majestic figure and penetrating stare that captured every scrap of her attention.

He'd changed too, and the traditional black and gold keffiyeh highlighted every streamlined angle and contour of his magnificent body. He didn't join in the dancing and clapping that was supposed to heap health and goodwill on them as a newly married couple. He simply watched her, compelling her closer with those eyes. And when she reached him, he took hold of her hand again, and together they walked to the throne-like chairs set up on a dais at the far end of the gargantuan ballroom.

Three hours later, Anaïs feared her smile was

permanently starched into place. She'd danced, sipped infrequently at her glass of vintage champagne and nibbled at exquisite food just so she wouldn't draw comment. But all evening the weighty ball in her stomach had steadily enlarged, turning from stone to lead as an unpleasant realisation revealed itself.

Her distant French relatives had left moments ago and Lauren, the only person she felt a genuine liking for, was across the room with her husband and Javid. The woman Javid had stiltedly introduced as his mother stood with another group nearby, and while Anaïs fleetingly pondered why Javid was actively ignoring her, why the older woman kept sliding longing glances towards him, the other matter sending bile to her throat all but consumed her.

Seizing the opportunity to escape for a few minutes, Anaïs excused herself with a polite smile from the group who, like many tonight, were subtly angling for her endorsement of one cause or another.

From the rehearsals, she knew there was one luxuriously appointed restroom reserved solely for her and Javid. She hurried towards the hallway leading to that blessedly quiet place, not entirely surprised when Faiza fell into step beside her.

'Is everything all right, Your Majesty?'

Anaïs swallowed and quickened her steps, eager

to rid her brain of what her eyes had clearly told her was happening.

Inside, she crossed to the sink and ran her wrists under cool water. When that didn't soothe her either, she turned to her assistant. 'That female head of state in the green gown, and the ambassador with red hair. They've both been involved with Javid, haven't they?' she asked through lips gone curiously numb.

Her eyes widened but, to her credit, Faiza didn't pretend ignorance. 'According to the media, yes, Your Majesty.'

Anaïs wanted to tell herself she was overblowing this. That she should overlook it. But hadn't she made the same mistake with Pierre? Ignored what was right under her nose until she'd become a laughingstock in their social circle?

'And the CEO in black?'

A wave of anxiety washing over her face, Faiza gave a short nod.

The roiling in her stomach intensified. 'Okay. You can go, Faiza.'

The younger woman lingered. 'Your Majesty…'

She forced a smile. '*C'est bon.* It's fine.'

Faiza opened her mouth again, then, with a soft sigh, she nodded and retreated, leaving Anaïs blessedly alone for the first time in hours.

Plucking the monogrammed towel, she distractedly dried her hands as the truth hammered through her brain.

Javid had invited his old flames to his...*their*... wedding.

Was that a signal that, marriage of convenience or not, he didn't intend to stop his sexual pursuits? Why, *oh, why* hadn't she insisted they have this conversation?

And what would she have said?

That she forbade him from doing so? That she would allow it *if* he was discreet?

The fierce flame of rejection that lit up in her at the second question gave her the answer. She tossed the towel away, then, unable to meet the hollow-eyed look in the mirror, she spun away.

Only to see the object of her chaotic thoughts striding into the restroom. Stunned, she watched Javid shut the door, decisively turn the bolt, then lean back against it, arms folded, those infernal eyes pinned on her.

Emotions fired up inside, a few of them absurdly inappropriate. Because his presence shouldn't be stirring anything besides prideful anger.

'What are you doing here?' she shot at him. How had he known she was here anyway? Surely Faiza hadn't given her away?

'If you're questioning your assistant's loyalty, don't. Her poker face, however, isn't one I'd stake empires on,' he said drolly.

The tiny bout of relief was snuffed out by his overwhelming presence. 'You haven't said what you're doing here. In case it's not obvious, I'm busy.'

His gaze trailed down her body, then rose to her face. 'I can see. Busy spitting acid and twisting your fingers into knots because…?' He let the question trail off, one eyebrow slowly elevating.

There were a dozen accusations she wanted to launch at him right now. Of course, the paramount one spilled free and frenzied when she wanted to remain composed and indifferent.

'You invited your paramours to *my* wedding?'

For the briefest moment, she knew what it felt like to surprise the unflappable King of Riyaal. His arms loosened and he jerked upright before adopting that indolent stance again.

With strides at once languid and animalistic, he approached. 'Excuse me?'

'You heard me well enough,' she snapped. 'I counted three of them, out there, drinking champagne and carrying on without a care in the world. Have you no shame?'

He shrugged, and the movement was entirely too distracting for her state of mind. 'Not in this case, *ma femme*.'

The impenitence of his answer rushed a red haze over her. For the first time in her life, Anaïs wanted to do physical harm to another. She wanted to pound his chest and claw at his face. That alone was enough to make her gasp. To make her realise that this was happening far too often with

Javid. His ability to trigger feverish emotions in her needed to be stopped.

She forced a cool nod. '*Tres bien.* In that case, I'll be sure to get Faiza to invite my exes the next time there is a state cere—'

His thick growl cut her off. She took a step back and found her back against a literal wall. His palms flattened on the wall on either side of her head, his body caging her without touching hers.

'Say that again,' he demanded, every trace of humour wiped from his rumbling tone.

Despite his proximity, his scent filling her nostrils and wreaking utter havoc on her senses, she met his gaze boldly. 'You keep asking me to repeat things. Are you hard of hearing, Your Majesty?'

A flash of teeth was lethal in its blinding and drew her eyes to his truly sumptuous, sculpted lips. Lips that looked even more sensually ruinous from this close. 'I thought you frigid when we first met. I'm happy to see it was all an act.'

She managed to scoff, her own lips curving in an indifferent smile. 'You think what you will. I don't give a—'

The rest of her words strangled in her throat when his lips slammed over hers.

This kiss was nowhere near as teasing or civil as the one in the cathedral had been.

From the very first touch, Javid punched passion and lust, intent and fever into the kiss. With one bold sweep of his tongue against the seam of her lips, her spine melted against the wall. He repeated the caress, slower, bolder, demanding entry.

And when Anaïs—against her better judgement but utterly helpless to resist him—gave her permission, he plunged deep, his exploration so thorough and masterful that she moaned, half in disbelief and half in the vortex of such need, she never wanted him to stop.

Mon Dieu, so this was what it felt like.

To be utterly undone by a kiss. Because in that moment, she couldn't have lifted a finger to change a single thing if her life depended on it. She wanted those hot, skilled, *sublime* lips to block out the outside world. Her hands to cling to those broad shoulders, to dig in harder and feel the rumble of his groan between their lips before they swallowed it down. For his body to press into hers in that magnificent way that felt like touching a pillar of flame; breathing it in until every pore was suffused with the stunning narcotic that was wild, unfettered desire.

The proud outline of his erection drew another whimper, another urgent dragging of her fingers through his hair, the heady feeling of power when he hissed against her lips, then groaned with satisfaction.

But it was that satisfaction…that vague echo of warning that she was playing right into his hands…that this was another means of conquest, that finally dragged her back to reality.

She ignored her body's screech of denial as she planted her fists on his shoulders and pushed him back.

'No.' Then, stronger, 'Stop.'

He pulled back instantly, and Anaïs desperately wished back the divine sensation of his body against hers. She might have stopped the kiss, but she couldn't avoid his wicked scrutiny of her face or the way his febrile eyes lingered on her kiss-bruised lips.

'There,' he breathed, his voice thick with lust and triumph. 'Now that's more like it.'

She drew in a shaky breath. 'M-more like what?'

'Our first kiss.'

'What are you talking about? You kissed me after we exchanged vows.'

He did that dismissive thing with his hand that was at once irritating and fascinating. 'That was something for the photos, not a real kiss.'

His gaze raked her face, taking in every inch of her reaction, every pulse racing at her throat with a look of unabashed male satisfaction. It was laughably primitive, and yet it punched another visceral hit of arousal through her pelvis.

'Now you look like you have been properly kissed. Not like that chaste bit of nonsense I barely felt at the ceremony.'

He'd barely felt that? When her lips still tingled after that faintest of touches?

Focus!

'If this is your way of trying to evade the subject we are discussing, it's not working.'

He raised one eyebrow, his gaze once again lingering far too long on her lips. 'If I was attempting evasion, my dear, you would know about it. There is no evasion.' His expression grew a touch hard and a lot serious. 'Those women are a part of my past but not inviting them would have caused more of a political headache than a few moments of your discomfort.'

She watched, wary and a little stunned, as he raised his hand, and drew his knuckles down her heated cheek. 'And for that, I have to beg your pardon. And your indulgence. We might need some of those figures somewhere down the road to aid us in Riyaali matters so it's best to keep them onside.'

Anaïs wasn't sure whether she was more stunned at his admission, his apology or the *'we'* tucked into that statement. All three combined to send a pulse of warmth through her that perhaps was unwise but still mellowed the roiling emotions within her.

She opened her mouth, but no words emerged. And it was possibly in that moment that she knew she was playing with a master of the game.

And he wasn't quite done.

Another transformation came over his face, his eyes narrowing into warning slits as his hand trailed down her neck, arm and wrist to rest at her waist. 'Now, to return to a more urgent subject. Be very careful what threats you issue. I do not share.'

'Don't you? Only news of your rampancy was well documented.'

'Don't confuse a robust but transient appetite with promiscuity.' His grip tightened. Not enough to bruise but enough to command her attention. As if she weren't rapt enough already. 'Past lovers are banned from your life. Permanently.'

'Let me guess. This is where you lay down rules that see you enjoying your extra-marital *liaisons* while I have to suffer—'

'*Suffer?* Why, *ma chérie*, that makes it sound almost like you care.'

'I care as much as you do. Which I'm guessing is very little.'

Something flickered in his eyes, wild and primal. But then the muffled sounds of laughter and intensified revelry trickled into their tight, turbulent space, reminding them where they were.

'On the contrary, I care very much,' he rasped. Then, in an edgier tone, 'So let me repeat myself. I don't share. Never have. Never will.'

'Then aren't you in the wrong job? Because you'll be sharing yourself with millions of subjects.'

'You're misunderstanding me. Deliberately, I suspect?'

She felt heat rising in her face. 'Am I?' She brazened it out.

'Na'am.' He growled the word for 'yes' in Arabic. 'For kingdom and duty, we will have no option but to devote our time and ourselves. Behind closed doors, I get you all to myself. No prevarications and no holding back. You're mine, Anaïs. Accept it now and we'll both have a smoother time of it.'

'And if I don't?' Why on earth was she so compelled to keep duelling with him?

Because you like it. Because it fires you up as nothing else has for a very long time.

She yearned to deny that all too knowing voice, but it rang far too true and far too frightening.

He'd drawn closer as her thoughts swirled like an impending tornado and with every second, he impacted her with the devastation of one. She couldn't breathe, couldn't look away.

Do you want to?

Enough.

'What a battle you're having with yourself.'

She swallowed and raised her chin. 'It's totally worth it if it means I never have to give in to you.'

'Ah, yet another challenge.' One masculine hand rose, and drifted slowly towards her, as if she were a skittish kitten he was taking time to calm. 'I look forward to drowning in this fever you seem immersed in.'

She felt her foolish eyes grow heavy, begin to drift shut at the enticement in his voice. She desperately tried to remain rigid. Removed. But, *mon Dieu*, she was only human. And the last time he'd touched her it'd been *incroyable*. So she let his knuckles drift down her hot cheek. Trail down to her jaw then redirect towards the corner of her mouth. She bit back a moan—because, for heaven's sake, she wasn't that far gone yet—and blinked up at him, attempting to show she wasn't a slave to this…insanity he initiated so freely.

Then he flipped his hand so the firm, slightly abrasive pads of his fingers came into play, drifting far too close to her lower lip, tracing the skin right beneath it. Making her flesh tremble.

A whimper broke free.

His nostrils flared, as if scenting a prey for weaknesses.

And she was weak. Weak with the need to sway closer. To capture that roving thumb between her lips, bite down with her teeth and make *him* moan.

No. Hadn't she talked herself into acting the exact opposite of what her senses were screaming at her to do now?

She cleared her throat and opened her mouth, just as he caught and meshed her fingers with his. Started to lift them up to his mouth as he'd done in the cathedral.

'What are you doing?'

He quirked a sleek eyebrow at her. 'Escorting my wife back to our wedding reception, what else?'

'But…we need to talk about something else.'

He shook his head. 'It can wait. We've neglected our guests for long enough.'

Still, she hesitated, that sensation of being on a slippery slope intensifying. 'If I walk out of here with you, everyone will know what we've been doing,' she said, her wildly tingling lips reminding her what they'd been doing.

Brushing her knuckles, he tucked her hand into his arm, his nostrils flaring with unabashed satisfaction. 'Good. Then they won't delay us when we tell them it's time for us to leave to enjoy our wedding night.'

CHAPTER FIVE

JAVID HAD PICKED Bora Bora as their honeymoon destination for three reasons.

The first was because the dossier he'd been given on his new wife mentioned it was number one on her bucket list.

The second reason—the murmurings of unrest back in Riyaal—he hoped would be resolved by the time they returned home in ten days.

The third—and currently gaining traction in urgency—was because he happened to have a paradise home there that would be the perfect scene for what he had in mind: picking up the gauntlet his wife had just thrown down.

He might have intended a strict non-carnal marriage of convenience when he'd accepted this role but that kiss in the bathroom, and the way Anaïs had responded to him, had opened a whole tantalising avenue of possibility. Besides, why suffer a prolonged life of celibacy when he didn't need to?

Javid wasn't a man who was consistently surprised, and yet Anaïs had repeatedly pulled the rug from under him in the past few weeks. That he hadn't been aware of the fullest extent of just what he was dealing with was his own fault.

That he hadn't discovered until after her crown was placed upon her head, declaring her Queen of Riyaal, that his new wife had no intention of sharing his bed, was only partially his fault.

That he intended to do something about that ridiculous declaration immediately…well, it was entirely his fault since he had never been able to resist a challenge.

'Let me get this straight. You intend for us both to lead celibate lives even though we've proved beyond a shadow of a doubt that we're compatible?'

A flare of heat had arisen in her cheeks after his stunned query.

'If you'd given me the time of day before the wedding when I requested it, you wouldn't be surprised now. Besides, it sounds like that was your intention too…before…what happened in the bathroom. There's no reason for it to change.'

His nostrils had flared in disbelief. 'You think not?'

She'd had the nerve to laugh. 'You really find that unconscionable, don't you? That a woman wouldn't want to sleep with you?'

'When that woman is my wife? *Na'am*,' he'd snarled, feelings roiling through him he'd hoped to have left behind years ago.

Bewilderment. Rejection.

He hadn't dealt with them well as a child. He'd learned to eliminate them in adulthood by the simple method of winning all the time. Only losers suffered rejection. Only chancers had to live with the risk of the unknown.

He planned. He strategised. And he won.

Except somehow, he'd stumbled into the unknown with Anaïs Dupont.

No, Anaïs Al-Riyaal. His queen, who wanted nothing to do with him on a personal level. 'I kissed you. And you enjoyed it.' Even in his own ears it had sounded far too insistent. A touch *desperate*. From a man who'd banned the word from his life from age ten.

'And that automatically means I want something more? That kiss was a mistake anyway. That's why I stopped it, remember?'

The regal set to her head, her very expression would've proclaimed her new status to the world had they not known it. He'd wisely refrained from pointing that out to her, lest her claws came out.

Perhaps that was why he'd had to re-strategise post-haste. He'd believed her cold and indifferent. He'd discovered she was anything but.

Her reaction to the unfortunate invitation of his exes, for instance. She'd been far from indifferent to that situation. That was a good starting point.

'*Na'am*, you stopped it. But not before you showed your hand, *ma chérie*.'

'What's that supposed to mean?'

'It means, we're going to be living far from the monastic existence you seem to have concocted in your head for us. If this was as important as you're making out it was, you should've made better efforts to get my attention.'

'You're saying it's on me that you made the baseless assumption that I would share your bed?' Her eyes had been alive with her incredulity.

'I'm saying that since you dropped the ball on something so fundamental, you should be prepared for talks to go a certain way.'

Her jaw had sagged for a moment, then that velvet mouth he couldn't stop thinking about had firmed. And he'd wanted to take it again, to press his tongue against that sensational seam and wait with bated breath for her to open for him.

The very idea that she'd given him—freely—that taste only to withhold further made that unwanted sensation tighten in his chest.

Rejection...

'*Tu n'es pas sérieux,*' she'd proclaimed hotly.

'*Jamais plus,*' he'd countered, again refraining from pointing out to her that she lapsed into French when her emotions were high. It was a... refreshing quality.

That was when their cool impasse had begun. Sure, she'd smiled and played newly-weds with him in public, but the moment they'd taken off on the royal jet, she'd found an excuse to disappear into the master suite.

He'd thought about going after her, but, for one thing, the very ferocity of his desire to change her mind had halted him in his tracks. Because winning was one thing, but this...*need* was quite another. He was a man who could take and leave as he pleased.

The notion that there was something else behind his thirst for conquest, something that perhaps harked back to his childhood isolation... disturbed him. Javid didn't like the fact that with Anaïs's outright refusal he'd had a snapshot of what the next ten years looked like. That the piercing need not to be adrift and alone in this new journey had triggered this quest.

For another thing he hadn't told her that the reason he'd been unavailable to meet with her before their wedding was because of the small but significant issue bubbling up. Javid's meeting with the head of one of Riyaal's most prominent families had made very little progress and both sides had walked away without a definitive resolution.

Javid exhaled his frustration as he paced the conference room on the plane. Concluding the meeting with his own advisors, he went into the main cabin and poured himself a drink. Bourbon in hand, he glanced at the closed door of the master suite.

He might have made little progress in one

arena, but he was damned if he would spend the next ten days taking the cold shoulder from his bride.

You should've made better efforts to get my attention.

Of all the heated words they'd exchanged, that one lingered longest, giving her pause before she condemned him outright for what should be an unjustified argument.

Because there were instances where she could've insisted he grant her five minutes to put this matter to bed. Hell, she could even have sent him an email. From his reaction, sending a message with the subject line *No sex in our marriage* would've grabbed his attention.

Had she subconsciously stalled this discussion? If so, why?

She flopped over on the king-sized bed, the drone of the plane's engines not doing a damned thing to calm nerves that had been stretched tight for what felt like days. Her churning mind refused to accept the possibility that she hadn't pushed as hard because she'd wanted a different outcome from what she'd rightly believed at the beginning: that this should be a sex-free marriage. At least for her.

Her stomach tightened in rejection of those last four words. She groaned again, burying her face in the pillow before giving in to the tiny scream trapped at the back of her throat.

She wasn't seriously debating this, was she? Tossing the pillow away, she rose and crossed to the stunningly appointed bathroom.

Despite being her late cousin's companion for a few years before the Queen had died, Anaïs had kept in the background, preferring to stay at home in the palace, for instance, rather than accompany her on the few foreign trips she'd taken. Which meant she hadn't been on the jet until today. Hadn't had an inkling of the supreme luxury and decadence of her surroundings and the sheer opulence that was her right now as Queen.

The Crown Jewels of Riyaal, for instance…

Anaïs shook her head, unwilling to think of all that now. Every facet of her life held such overwhelming weight she feared she would crumble beneath it if she wasn't careful.

Instead, she thought of their destination as she straightened her clothes and reapplied her pale lipstick.

Bora Bora.

Formerly a dream big destination on her bucket list, now chosen by her husband as their honeymoon destination.

Again…why?

She growled her frustration and left the bathroom. She didn't plan on arriving with this matter unresolved between them. It was time to tackle it once and for all.

An elegantly dressed attendant directed her to a door just past the main cabin. Sucking in a breath, she knocked.

'Yes?'

She ignored the shiver that ran through her at the sound of Javid's deep voice. Entering, she saw him seated at the head of a conference table, papers strewn in front of him. The bespoke jacket and tie he'd worn for their departure from the palace were discarded, leaving him in a midnight-blue shirt unbuttoned at the neck with his sleeves rolled up.

His hair was sexily tousled, the result of running his fingers through it, and from this short distance the impressive breadth of his shoulders was entirely too absorbing. And when he moved to stand, she clenched her belly to halt the rush of heat to her body, the tight furling of her nipples and sweet ache commencing between her thighs.

The urge to turn around and lock herself back in the master suite was strong. But, *zut*, she wasn't going to give him the satisfaction of knowing how deeply he affected her.

So she moved forward, her breath snagging dangerously when he rounded the table and prowled towards her.

'I think we need to talk, settle this thing once and for all.'

His nod made the muted lights overhead dance over his lustrous hair. Recalling how it'd felt to sink her fingers into the strands didn't help matters so she dragged her gaze away.

He waved her towards a grouping of club chairs near the left bank of windows. 'I agree. Would you like a drink?'

She followed his gaze to the side cabinet displaying a vast array of drinks. Her knee-jerk instinct was to refuse but she didn't want to start this by being discourteous. *'Oui, merci,'* she murmured, then cringed inwardly.

A few short strides and he was expertly tossing ice cubes into a glass and concocting a drink. Her eyes widened when he strode towards her with what looked like a cognac spritzer in his hand. Her favoured drink. 'How do you know...?'

'I'd hardly make an effective diplomat or ruler if I didn't do my homework, would I?' he drawled.

She accepted the drink with a flare of panic. If he'd done his homework, did he know why she'd left Paris? Know about Pierre?

She watched him retrieve his own glass and take the seat across from her, arranging himself in that lazy sprawl that drew her attention to the play of muscles in his thighs.

Hastily taking a much-needed sip of her drink, she set it to the side and plunged right in. 'I have no interest in sleeping with you. But even if I did, you'll agree that the circumstances of this...agreement would make the subject of sex just another complication we don't need?'

For several seconds, he remained silent, one finger rimming his glass. 'Are you trying to convince yourself or me?' he replied, his eyes hooded and his tone a low, deep rumble that drew her focus to every inch of her skin.

'I'm already convinced. You're the one who made assumptions,' she returned, that heat spreading wider through her.

'So what you're proposing is no sex for the foreseeable future. For either of us?' Another dangerous rumble, reminiscent of an awakening volcano. 'Isn't that an unnecessarily...lonely prospect?'

Anaïs gave a soft gasp. She'd expected this conversation to go many places, but not here. Not with this...raw admission. By the frown creasing his brow, she suspected neither had Javid. She opened her mouth to scoff at it, but different words tumbled out. 'Are you saying that you don't want to be alone?' she asked in a hushed voice.

Something tightened in his face, and she realised that him admitting such a thing would be revealing himself as human. As flesh and blood with feelings that an ordinary being possessed.

And yet, it was there, shrouded behind the fiercely proud and arrogant veneer. She knew what it looked like because she too felt it. In her darkest nights she knew she'd fled France to Riyaal because she'd needed the comfort of her friendship with Yasmin. She'd needed to not be so...*alone*.

His gaze dropped to his glass for a moment before meeting hers. 'I'm saying that alliances are always better than going it alone. You want a peaceful and prosperous Riyaal, so do I. For the sake of our respective cousins, don't we owe it to them to try?'

'But I'm already your queen. We're already... united, *non*?'

Now the cynicism made an appearance. 'Façades wear thin. And they harden and break eventually.'

'What are you saying, Javid?'

His nostrils flared briefly, and he seemed to ponder his words carefully before he replied. 'I'm saying that rather than battle for the sake of it, let's use this time to let this happen...naturally. I'm confident it will aid us better in what lies ahead.'

She swallowed, a combination of alarm and anticipation writhing through her. 'Emotional and physical trial and error? Is that what you're proposing instead of leaving our emotions out of this altogether?'

One corner of his mouth lifted. 'No matter how much we like to think our entanglements are emotionless there is a base line of trust and at least a little connection, isn't there?'

Her heart lurched. 'If I didn't know better, I'd say you just admitted you might like me.'

The sardonic mockery she'd expected didn't come. Nor did he deny it. He just gave another of those expressive shrugs. 'You…intrigue me. Two weeks ago, I'd have sworn I was unaffected. But I'm man enough to admit it isn't so. Just as I'm admitting to you that the road ahead is tough without adding unnecessary obstacles to it.'

You intrigue me.

To anyone else, it would've been a run-of-the-mill compliment to take or leave.

To plain, boring, virgin Anaïs, it was a heart-leaping moment she wanted to reject immediately the sensation assailed her. Because it was daunting. And exhilarating. But she didn't. Couldn't. Because again, she sensed the weight behind his admission.

Or was she deluding herself?

Too late, she was equally stirred by the possibility. More than stirred. Losing Yasmin had removed her last friend and confidante. She didn't fool herself into thinking Javid would fill that role. But if he came even close to removing that sensation of being…alone? Available, but perhaps not needed? Wouldn't that make this new, fearful role easier to bear?

Another circuit of his finger around the rim of the glass as leonine eyes, made more hypnotic by the slanting of the sunlight through the jet's windows, watched her.

Something about the calm and meticulous way he was laying out his argument was…intoxicating—

He broke into her thoughts by continuing. 'Be bold, Anaïs. Consider my offer. But don't wait too long. In front of staff and guests and the general public, we will continue as we have been. I will touch you. Who knows? Maybe you'll crave my kisses too. But nothing stays secret for ever, especially within palace walls. We have enough eyes on us not to toss in speculation of why we're not sharing a bed.'

He slowly surged upright, his stance no longer laid-back. 'I suspect neither of us want to be the subject of endless gossip and at least a dozen unauthorised biographies speculating on our sex life even before my first year of rule is up.'

She waved away his absurd answer. *'Tu exagéres.'*

For some reason her response drew momentary amusement. Then his features grew serious. 'Do I? You forget my status before our current situation. I know first-hand what it feels like to live in the public eye as a prince. Trust me, the things you see and read about in the tabloids are just the tip of the iceberg when it comes to how deep the media will dig to find a crumb of scandal. Why put ourselves through that if we don't have to?'

'You didn't seem to be that considerate when you were single.'

He tilted his head, one eyebrow slowly rising. 'And that doesn't tell you anything?'

The feeling that oozed through her only added to her confusion. Surely, he wasn't implying that…she had been the catalyst for this change?

You intrigue me.

That brought her up short. She was used to thinking of him as the playboy or the diplomat, but she rarely thought of him as the prince. From the bitter twist to his lips, it dawned on her that there was a whole other facet to this man she had very little idea about.

What was his favourite pet growing up?

Who was his best friend at school?

What did he—?

Pour l'amour de Dieu! Focus!

Or next she'd be contemplating what it was like to be his friend. What it would be like to share their hopes and dreams.

She pursed her lips. 'So, I'm to allow you to paw me in public for the sake of this…charade?' She hit out, knowing the argument was perhaps unfair and half-hearted at best.

His face hardened, the haughty clench to his jaw reminding her that he was of royal blood, forged from the steel and pride of marauders. 'I remember only one of us doing the pawing in that bathroom, *habibti*. You'll be happy to know I wasn't displeased by it.'

Flames shot into her cheeks. 'I told you, that was unintended.'

'Pity. It could be an excellent prologue to our story.'

'I…' She floundered, shook her head. 'This isn't how I—'

'Expected this to go?' he finished for her. 'Things rarely do. The trick is to ensure you leave the table with more than you arrived with.'

She'd been in Riyaal long enough to see Yasmin's irritation when the media had blown the smallest thing out of proportion. The last thing she needed was for them to dig into her past; for Yasmin's memory to be tainted by the exposition of Anaïs's dirty laundry in the form of her playboy ex-fiancé.

More than that, she hated the idea of stepping into her cousin's shoes while fronting a lie.

Sure, she and Javid would never be star-crossed lovers, but did they have to be bitter enemies? Especially now when he'd lowered his own guard, even by a small fraction?

As long as she strictly guarded her heart, could they lay down their arms and make this work?

She eyed him, tried to see beneath the steady look he levelled on her. 'I agree. Within reason and at my own pace.'

'Na'am,' he rumbled, the glint of satisfaction in his eyes unmistakable.

'You're very pleased with yourself, aren't you?'

A hard little smile winked in and out. 'No, *chère femme*. Pleased would be receiving your wholesome and wholehearted agreement. But I get that things didn't happen conventionally between us. I'm patient enough to wait you out.'

She tilted her chin. 'You might be waiting for a long time.'

'Perhaps,' he drawled, so sure of himself that her fingers clenched in alarm in her lap. 'But the wait will be worth it.'

The attendant's knock to announce that they would be landing in fifteen minutes ended their discussion.

Javid rose and held out his hand to her.

Acutely aware that the attendant hovered nearby, and equally aware of the agreement she'd just given, she accepted his hand. Let him lead her into the main cabin and usher her into the long sofa. Endured his blinding smile and his ministration as he secured her seat belt before tending to his own.

And when, after they landed on a private strip on the largest of a secluded chain of islands, he murmured, 'Wait for me,' she acquiesced, watched him stride to retrieve his jacket; got the first taste of what it felt like not to fight with Javid every second of every day.

A little nonplussed by the sensation, she watched him shrug it on with smooth sophistication, the outline of his torso and shoulders moulded against his shirt drying every square inch of her mouth.

And once done and they were leaving the jet, his hand found the small of her back as he escorted her off the plane and into the first of three SUVs waiting to drive them away. Through the light halter-neck top she'd paired with her wide palazzo pants, his hand burned her skin, sending further waves of heat through her body that had nothing to do with the dazzling sunlight that greeted them.

She hid behind wide designer shades all the way through wrought-iron gates and up a short tree-lined driveway to the most spectacular wooden villa she'd ever seen.

A skilled cross between Polynesian and European, it sat on three levels, and, even from the driveway, Anaïs spotted the abundance of terraces and open spaces.

The dozen-strong staff stood at the front entrance to greet them, their expressions a cross between familiar friendliness and awe. The distant buzz that set off was lost beneath the splendour of the interior.

Dark and rich polished wood were juxtaposed with white walls and colourful paintings. It wasn't the opulence of the Riyaal royal palace or even the sophistication of the private jet, but it more than held its own in natural beauty and elegance, every room decked out with sumptuous, premium comfort in mind in the form of plush sofas, cosy lamps and eye-catching sculptures.

And on the outside, hammocks and plat-formed decks and cabanas with billowing mus-lin drapes.

After years of wistful wishing, Anaïs could scarcely believe she was finally here. Of course, the reason for her presence in this place wasn't easy to dismiss, especially when Javid drew close once their housekeeper had drifted away to see to their luggage.

'Is it meeting your bucket-list expectations yet?'

'More than…' She trailed off when his words seeped in. 'Wait, you know about my bucket list?'

'Of course. Why else did you think the itiner-ary was altered?'

'Where were we going originally?'

'I have a weakness for the Seychelles. But we can go there another time.'

The clink of ice cubes drew her attention to the butler, who bore a tray of refreshments.

'Thank you, Nathan.'

The brown-skinned butler flashed a dazzling smile at Javid. 'My pleasure, Your Majesty. And on behalf of the staff, I'd like to say how good it is to have you back with us.'

'Thank you,' Javid repeated with a smile of his own.

The familiarity between them turned the puzzling buzz into enlightenment. 'You've been here before, haven't you?'

'A few times, yes.'

'Do you own this villa?'

'Yes. And the island, which are both yours now too.' Oblivious to the shocking import of his words, he handed her a colourful turquoise drink, complete with a cute little umbrella, then clinked his own, less playful glass against hers. 'To our more…amenable alliance.'

Try as she might, she couldn't shake off the kindling effect of those words. Nor could she stop him from touching her—the inside of her wrist to slow her down before a painting, the small of her back to usher her into a room, her ear as he tucked a strand of hair behind her it—as they toured the rest of the house.

Anaïs was actively willing the tour to be over by the time the housekeeper showed them into a breathtaking suite on the corner of the west wing. The theme of white walls and furnishings blended with dark, polished teak and highlighted with bursts of brightness made her want to shed her travel clothes at the first opportunity and plunge into holiday mode.

Through French doors, a double-wide hammock swayed gently in the breeze, with several lounge chairs inviting relaxation. But what made her breath catch all over again was the half-Olympic-sized pool, sparkling an inviting turquoise beneath the mid-afternoon sun.

As if he'd read her thoughts, Javid strode out onto the terrace to join her. 'Meet me by the pool in an hour?'

She bit her inner lip. Within reason and at her own pace. It was just a swim, so why did it make her stomach dip and dance?

'Don't overthink it, *ma chérie*. It's just a chance to relax after our long journey.' His gaze flitted to her bedroom, and massive four-poster bed waiting invitingly behind her. 'You don't want to go to bed now, or you'll be up all night with jet lag.'

And because she couldn't find an argument to counter that, she answered, *'Bien sûr.'*

'Good. Until then.' Thinking he would exit the way they'd come in—through her private living room—she frowned when he strolled to the far side of the terrace, and another set of French doors.

'What…where are you going?'

He threw her an arrogant smile over her shoulder, his expression not in the least bit repentant. 'Our suites are connected by a joint terrace.' He nudged his head towards the entrance. 'My doors are always open. Feel free to use them.'

Anaïs was still blinking in stunned surprise, unsure whether to be alarmed or outraged, when he disappeared into his own suite.

Any chance of gaining any semblance of calm

evaporated when she re-entered her own suite. The thought that they were separated by a mere wall dangled her on tenterhooks for the whole time the staff unpacked her luggage in the spacious dressing room adjoining her luxurious bathroom.

The sensation remained once she was alone. She paced, unable to settle. She'd agreed to choosing harmony over strife in both their public and private lives, for the sake of Riyaal and their respective cousins' memories.

But that didn't mean she was a walkover now, as she'd been with Pierre. Javid clearly excelled at negotiation. She could keep scrambling to keep up with him. Or she could step up to his level.

She paused in the middle of her bedroom, a tiny smile teasing the corners of her mouth. Rather than be repeatedly caught off guard, she'd simply take the wind out of his sails.

The thought steeped in her brain, gaining momentum as she changed into a lemon-yellow bikini and matching, floaty sundress made of the softest chiffon.

Her years in Riyaal had lent her skin a golden tan, which set off the colour satisfactorily. She brushed her hair out, donned stylish sunglasses and slipped her feet into gold platform mules.

A hovering attendant smilingly ushered her down a series of hallways and out onto the terrace leading to the sparkling pool. She breathed a sigh of relief to see she was first out. Choosing a cushioned lounger, she accepted an ice-cold fruit punch from a staff member.

She'd just taken her first sip when she realised she'd forgotten her suncream. She wrinkled her nose in annoyance, just as a low deep voice rumbled over her.

'The drinks aren't that bad, surely?' Javid asked.

Aware of the hovering staff, and unwilling to cause offence, she shook her head instantly. 'Of course not. They're delicious.'

'Then what's the problem?' he pushed as he took the seat next to her.

Anaïs couldn't stop her gaze from devouring him. In her defence, there was a lot to appreciate about him. Especially since he wore a pair of designer swim shorts, the customary Vacheron Constantin watch he rarely took off, and not much else. A wide expanse of sculpted torso and ripped muscles snagged at least half a minute of her attention, the wisps of hair arrowing from the middle of his chest to his waistband, and beyond, creating a hunger in her belly that almost made her moan out loud.

Thankfully, she curbed the sound as he stretched out like a feline predator on the lounger, corded arms folding behind his head and his face turned towards her as he awaited her answer. Even though he wore shades, she felt the laser-beam focus of his eyes.

She swallowed past the thickness in her mouth. 'I'm annoyed with myself because I forgot to bring my sunscreen, that's all.'

'You have over a dozen staff members at your disposal who would be happy to get you what you need,' he said.

'I'm not really comfortable with people fetching and carrying for me.'

His face grew serious. 'Get comfortable with it. You're a queen now, Anaïs. A certain behaviour is expected. Besides, you have more important things to be doing than running back and forth with jobs other people are employed to do for you.'

She pressed her lips together but before she could answer, he was continuing.

'Remember that, even here, everyone has their designated positions. Start straying into and usurping, albeit unintentionally, other people's and you not only risk making them feel insecure, you also risk cultivating resentment.'

'I...never quite thought of it that way,' she murmured, annoyed with herself all over again.

He quirked a smile. 'This can be the beginning of our harmonious cooperation.'

The idea that this could actually work, that she could pull off being Queen, kicked deep emotion inside her.

With Javid at her side, this weight might not be so heavy—

The thought stuttered to a halt when he lifted one arm and languidly beckoned one of the female staff. He murmured to her and received a nod and smile in return.

A different sort of sensation took hold, a mild churning in the pit of her stomach that bewildered and irritated. 'Do you set out to charm every female in sight or is it just when I'm around?'

He stilled and one eyebrow arched above the top frame of his sunglasses. 'Are you jealous, *ma petite*?' he drawled, amusement etched into the words.

'Not at all. Just asking what I should be watching out for in the future, that's all.'

He took his time to pluck his shades off his face and toss them onto the nearby table. Then he subjected her to the full blast of those leonine, mesmeric eyes.

'Put your claws away, *habibti*. I'm currently fascinated by one woman only.'

Several new emotions bombarded her. The need to immunise herself against his casual use of endearments; the fact that she'd exhibited her jealousy so blatantly; but it was that 'currently' that sparked further churning through her.

Harmonious cooperation or not, he'd just reminded her what sort of man he was. She sucked in a slow breath, reminding herself of the need to guard her deeper emotions at all costs.

When the female member of staff—whose name she recalled as Gemmie—returned with a basket containing at least a dozen far superior sunscreen brands to the one Anaïs normally used, she smiled her thanks, set her drink down and, rising, shed her dress.

She heard Javid's sharp intake of breath but didn't glance his way. Instead, she turned away, attempting not to blush or die of self-consciousness at his ferocious scrutiny, as Gemmie took her dress to hang it on a hook nearby, before quickly making herself scarce once Javid assured her they didn't need anything else.

Bending over, Anaïs pretended an avid interest in selecting a bottle.

Her bikini wasn't immodest, but it was, well… a bikini. Which meant the globes of her breasts and bottom were blatantly moulded by the stretchy material, the yellow further highlighting the smoothness of her skin.

Her choice in hand, she straightened, dragged the curtain of her hair over one shoulder to find Javid upright, his eyes fixed squarely on her.

One hand extended commandingly. 'Here, let me.' His voice was thick and husky, his nostrils set at a distinct flare when he inhaled again.

Anaïs reminded herself she couldn't back down now, even though the ever-present heat when he was in close proximity had ignited into a conflagration.

'Of course.' She held out the tube of waterproof sunscreen. Then, once he took it from her, added, 'As long as I get to return the favour.'

Wary surprise flickered through his eyes, and she silently congratulated herself, secretly pleased with nudging, if not completely pulling, the rug from under his feet.

'How can I refuse an offer like that from my wife?' he returned, his voice still thick and throbbing with strong currents that made the muscles in her stomach quake. Firm, bronze hands wrapped around the bottle; he conducted a slow, top-to-toe appraisal of her body. Then, still holding her gaze, he rasped, 'Lie down.'

Anaïs was more than happy to sink back onto the lounger, the power of his scrutiny having weakened her knees.

He watched her for several long seconds, then in one smooth lunge he'd moved to the bottom of her seat. Flicking the lid of the suncream open, he squirted a dollop into his hand.

Her heart started to thunder as his gaze drifted down her body. One large hand wrapped around her ankle, drawing up her leg. He planted her foot on his chest and her breath quaked in her lungs.

Mon Dieu, he'd barely touched her and already she was... *No, she was stronger than this.*

She tried not to let the sensation of his rippling

pectoral muscles beneath her foot unsettle her. But then his hand was smoothing the cream over the top of her foot, his touch unhurried as he worked the substance into her skin. Rather than hold her gaze the way he'd been doing relentlessly for the last few minutes, Javid seemed enthralled by his actions, his gaze following the glide of his fingers. Watching him watch her was surprisingly and intensely sexy, the action flaming more heat through her.

By the time she'd turned over and he'd smoothed his hands over her bottom, back and was retracing them down the curve of one hip, Anaïs was desperately trying not to pant, not to let Javid's own faintly erratic breathing, clenched features and a swathe of colour high on his chiselled cheekbones affect her.

This was the reaction she'd been aiming for: for him not to underestimate her. Steeping that reminder in her mind, she bit the inside of her lower lip, schooled her features and drew her hair over one shoulder to peer at him. '*Merci.* I think it's your turn now.'

He dragged his gaze from her backside, his features still clamped in tight emotion and his eyes smouldering brighter. She caught a flicker of warning in his eyes. Then it was gone, and he was rising, stretching out on his own lounger, a panther in his domain.

Girding her heated loins, Anaïs shakily retrieved the sunscreen, and sent a silent prayer that she got through this without turning herself inside out with this game she'd embroiled herself in.

CHAPTER SIX

JAVID SUSPECTED HIS wife was attempting to hoist him with his own petard. The memory of how smooth, silky and warm her skin had felt under his touch flamed through his veins even as he bit back a groan when her hands moved over his shoulders. If this was what she meant by within reason and at her own pace, he wasn't going to protest. Because if that meant more of this…

He gritted his teeth and mentally shook his head.

She was already growing far too addictive far too quickly.

Forging an easier alliance so the ten years of his reign wouldn't be entirely unbearable was one thing. Letting her win, even at something as ephemeral as sex, was quite another.

There was a reason he'd trained himself never to be in the thrall of a woman. They were mercurial creatures. Like his mother, their affection waxed and waned like the lunar cycle, more often than not entirely tied into what they could gain from him. What his regal status could bring them.

He'd trained himself to give only so much and no more. To take what he wanted and, while ensuring both parties were satisfied, to never stay long enough to be used or rejected. To never be made to feel as if he was surplus to requirements after he'd worn out his usefulness.

While, contrarily, he'd made himself indispensable to the people that mattered to him. Rewarded loyalty with loyalty. If he could count those people on the fingers of one hand, then so be it. He'd rather have that than thousands of acolytes who would only take and take.

Whatever Anaïs was offering, he needed to match like for like and no more. As long as it benefited Riyaal, and a harmonious kingdom, of course. Adnan had been misguided, but he'd loved his kingdom. Javid owed it to his flesh and blood not to falter in his rule.

So he clenched his gut against the surge of lust as her fingers glided over his triceps, and reminded himself that, only a few hours ago, Anaïs had been adamantly opposed to this. To have changed her mind so quickly…

Could he trust her?

No matter.

His guard would stay high. He'd see where she intended to take this. And if it ended up with her in his bed…

'Est-ce bon?' Is this okay?

He hid his smile because once again she'd given herself away with that husky query in her father tongue.

'I'm not complaining,' he returned, letting amusement trail through his response even as the unsettled sensation remained. It'd been a long time since he'd felt even remotely out of his depth.

But then he'd never held the role of King. Never had to take a wife. All new situations that justified his current mood, surely?

No.

The challenges of ruling were unique enough to hold his interest, the idea of forging a better path for Riyaal and its people on the world stage one he'd quickly grown to relish.

In ten years, he would hand over the reins to whoever succeeded him with a much better kingdom than his late cousin had left it.

As for his wife and queen…

He would let her in. Up to a point. No more.

'Turn over.'

He complied, ignoring the echoes of hollowness in his stomach as he settled onto his back and watched the flush of arousal creep across her cheeks. Pure male satisfaction oozed through him as her eyes zeroed in on his stiff shaft before quickly glancing away, triggering that notion of innocence.

It didn't matter how fascinating he found that, either. Like all things, this too would wear off.

So he folded his arms behind his head, not bothering to hide her effect on him as her hands trailed over his chest, his thighs and calves. Watched her heated cheeks grow into a full-blown blush.

'It was inevitable, *chérie*. Just as it was for you.' He deliberately glanced at her chest, where her nipples stood to attention.

She jerked off the lounger as if scalded, her movements coltish but still puzzlingly graceful as she plucked off her sunglasses and tossed them onto the table. 'I'm going for a swim.'

Ignoring the throb of hunger in his groin that demanded immediate satisfaction with this woman who made his blood roar in his veins, the clamour to glide his tongue over those nipples, to suck and tease until she cried out in his arms, he rose.

'I'll join you. I think we both need to cool off before things get too much out of hand, no? We wouldn't want to scandalise our staff on our very first day here.'

Her lips pursed but she didn't offer any argument as he followed her to the edge of the pool. Without glancing his way, she executed a neat dive, her slim body scything through the water with strong strokes that took her halfway before she emerged. Still not looking his way, she swam to the end, then braced herself with her arms on the tiles.

Javid dived in, thankful for the cool water and hoping it would help him gain some clarity or cool the raging hunger prowling through him. It didn't.

She'd turned towards him by the time he reached her, even though there was a stiffness to her shoulders when she faced him.

'What is the plan here? That we swim and laze about for the next ten days? Only I don't think I can do that.'

'Why not? When was the last time you had a proper holiday?'

She frowned. 'I don't remember.'

'There's your answer, then.'

Her eyes narrowed, as if she suspected a sting in his offer. Once again, Javid wondered who had made her so suspicious. Then he shrugged it away. Everyone was entitled to their baggage.

So why was the notion of letting her keep hers so abhorrent to him?

'And you? Are you planning on just topping up your tan while you're here?'

'No. Unfortunately, I'm far too driven to be content with doing one thing at a time.'

Her eyes widened, and that blush started to creep back into her cheeks.

He let out a low laugh. 'That wasn't meant to be sexually suggestive, *chère femme*, but I'm glad to see you're not above having a one-track mind.'

'I wasn't…you don't know what I was thinking!'

'Don't I?' Raising a hand, he trailed wet knuckles down her cheek. 'This gives you away quite conclusively.'

She jerked away, crossing one arm over her chest while attempting to keep herself afloat with the other. 'The only person with a one-track mind here is you.'

He *tsked*. 'Let's not argue in front of the staff. Not unless you're not averse to making up in front of them, too?'

She went from affronted to contemplative in mesmerising degrees.

Javid could almost see her mind ticking over with the precision of a Swiss clock, the connotations of his holding her in thrall as her arms dropped from her chest.

Then she floored him again by doing the unexpected.

Raising her own hand, she mirrored his gesture, the soft pads of her fingers tracing over his jaw. Making his abdominal muscles clench fiercely as her touch zapped electricity through his blood.

'*Bien sûr, mon cher.*' Her fingers crept further back and curled into the hair at his nape. 'I agree, it would be unseemly to give the staff the impression that we don't like each other,' she murmured, a curious bite in her voice.

Javid reckoned he would've been made of stone not to reach for her, not to settle his hands at her waist and pull her closer. Not to angle his head in anticipation of tasting those Cupid's bow lips dotted with moisture.

She relocated her hand, her fingers settling on his lips. To anyone watching, it would've looked as if she were still caressing him. But the firm pressure was a warning to halt.

Far from being irritated, he found the move excited him even further, the thrill of this particular chase unlike anything he'd experienced before. Going one better, he parted his lips and caught her middle finger between his teeth.

She inhaled sharply, her beautiful eyes darkening as he flicked his tongue against her flesh.

'I'm still waiting to hear plans of our activities.'

He wanted to order her into his bed then and there. Command her not to leave it for the next ten days except for food. But for one thing, he wasn't a primitive bastard, plus he'd have a riot on his hands if he even suggested such a thing. For another, he was curious to see where she was going with this.

With another flick of his tongue, he released her, another surge of need pummelling him when her eyes dropped to his mouth before meeting his.

'I've organised a sunset cruise for us tonight. It's a great way to see the other islands. As for tomorrow and the days after, I'll have to juggle some governing with our time here, but your time will be mostly yours to do with as you please.'

One delicate eyebrow arched. 'Mostly?'

'*Na'am*. I'll need you occasionally. We have an agreement, remember?'

A shadow eased over her features and had he been dealing with anyone else, Javid would've thought she was disappointed by his response. Her expression cleared a moment later, though, that infernal composure, which would be useful when dealing with state affairs but irritated the hell out of him when dealt to him personally, sliding into place.

'Of course,' she replied.

For a scant moment, he wished she'd said that in French, just so he'd know it was laced with emotion. But wasn't emotion, especially *false* emotion, something he'd vowed to distance himself from? Swearing silently at the confounding sensations buffeting him, he rustled up a smile.

'Good. I think another half-hour out here should do it for this afternoon.'

Turning, he forced himself to swim away, to vault out of the pool and return to the lounger. To don his glasses and watch her swim a few more lengths, probably in a bid to avoid him, before rising like a goddess from the water. Hardest of all, Javid tried not to ogle her like an uncouth schoolboy as she plucked up a towel and dabbed extra moisture off her lithe, supple body, tried not to call *to hell with it* and turn up the seduction level to one hundred just so he could get his hands on those luscious curves and valleys.

He succeeded by the skin of his teeth.

And when she joined him for light refreshments, he kept the conversation light, giving her a brief history of the island, his acquisition and construction of the villa. Anything else but the high-voltage awareness arcing between them.

It was with part relief, part disgruntlement that he brushed a kiss over her cheek half an hour later, assuring himself that it was for the sake of their audience, not because he yearned to feel her smooth skin against his for an instant.

'Duty calls. I'll come and collect you in three hours,' he said.

Then he walked away.

Javid didn't come to collect her in three hours.

A smiling Gemmie, who apparently also doubled up as a stylist and had helped her two personal attendants get Anaïs ready, informed her that His Majesty had been called away on another call minutes before he was supposed to meet her. So Anaïs was to meet him at the jetty instead.

She wanted to be irritated but, deep down, she was thankful for the extra few minutes granted her before she faced Javid again.

Because this afternoon hadn't gone quite the way she'd hoped. Or…more accurately…it'd gone a little too well.

Anaïs couldn't deny that she affected Javid on a base level, that the feminine power trailing through her veins even now, hours later, was a realisation that could prove dangerous if not contained. Because she'd revelled in his unguarded reaction to her touch; had wanted to keep stoking that fire long after her point was made.

It was only after he'd walked away that she'd registered that she'd...*enjoyed* it on some level.

Which said what about her?

She pressed her lips together and Gemmie peered at her. 'Are the diamonds not to your satisfaction, Your Majesty?'

She forced herself to smile. 'Can we settle on another name, Gemmie? Just while I'm here?'

Gemmie smiled—the woman seemed incapable of not smiling. 'Just between us? Maybe. Is "madam" better?'

Anaïs sighed and nodded. 'Please.'

'Okay, madam. Now, are we going to be fashionably late or terribly late?' she asked with a grin. 'Only, you need to make a decision on whether you're going with the diamonds or the emeralds.'

Anaïs looked down at her dress. It was another floaty number, similar to the sundress she'd worn earlier, but with a little more style that lent itself to evening wear. She loved it because its off-the-shoulder style and thigh slits wouldn't be too stifling in Bora Bora's sultry heat.

Meeting Gemmie's gaze in the mirror, she nodded at the emeralds. They were the less blingy of the two, one large stone in the middle with two smaller stones on either side, they were linked with a white platinum chain and came with matching teardrop earrings.

Her attendants had been mildly horrified when she'd suggested going without jewellery at all. Hell, she'd have advocated slipping into another swimsuit with a wrap and going barefoot but apparently queens didn't do that.

A touch of rebellion fizzed through her.

Maybe it was time to start her own tradition…

Despite the thought, she accepted that she loved the feel of the dress and the sophistication of the jewellery as she followed another staff member out of the villa and down a winding flower-lined pathway to the wide jetty.

There a tender waited and when they'd left the shore Anaïs searched the horizon for their destination, her jaw dropping when she caught glimpse of the vessel anchored about a mile away.

The superyacht was sleek but immense, easily one hundred metres long, its dark grey lines trimmed with silver, with multiple decks that would take at least several hours to fully explore.

Several bodyguards were positioned at strategic points around the yacht, reminding her of Javid's and her status. Apparently, even a sunset cruise on an idyllic island in Bora Bora didn't come without security concerns.

And right at the topmost deck, his feet braced apart while he conducted a phone call next to the railing, was Javid.

The flare of awareness over her skin told her he was watching her. That sensation continued as she was helped off the tender and another member of staff came forward with a smile and bow.

'Welcome aboard, Your Majesty. Please, follow me.'

A few minutes later, she stepped onto the deck.

Javid was still on the phone, his face set in severe lines as he spoke in rapid-fire Arabic. As she drew closer, he ended the call and handed the phone to another staff member, who immediately whisked it out of sight.

She trailed to a stop in the middle of the deck, the sheer impact of his presence slowing her feet. He didn't have any such qualms though. He advanced until he was half a foot from her, then he lowered his head and brushed a kiss along her jaw, sending tiny fireworks skittering throughout her body.

She scrambled for composure when she stepped back by pretending to examine her surroundings.

'When you mentioned a sunset cruise, I thought you meant a small boat not…this,' she said, desperate to defuse the charge that had resurged between them so effortlessly, it was almost as if their hours apart—and the severe self-admonition—hadn't had a single impact.

'You disapprove?' he asked, one eyebrow raised.

Did she? As with the title and the jewels and the private jet, she knew her new station in life was one of immense wealth and privilege. Was she going to keep railing at a situation that had been in place for decades, perhaps even centuries?

'Not necessarily,' she responded eventually.

He gave a satisfied nod. 'Good.'

'Isn't it a *faux pas* to come aboard a vessel like this with shoes on?'

He shrugged. 'When you own the vessel, you can do as you please.' His response was carefree enough, but tension remained in his shoulders and in faint lines around his mouth.

Recalling that he'd rearranged their meeting place because of a phone call, she frowned inwardly, wondering whether to enquire about it or not.

He was the King. He had a whole council of advisors to deal with whatever the latest challenge was. But they'd agreed to take this path together. To lean on one another, unify in rule when necessary.

So she took a breath. 'What was that about just now?'

He tensed slightly. 'I don't want to bore you with state matters.'

'It's my state now too, as you keep reminding

me. So?' she pressed after accepting the cocktail a server brought to her on a sterling silver tray.

For several moments, he remained silent. Then his gaze flicked to the staff members on the deck. Heeding the silent command, they filed out.

Once they'd made themselves scarce, Javid caught her elbow in a light hold and led her to the railing edging the deck.

The yacht glided through the waters with barely a ripple, and had she not been standing near the edge she wouldn't have known they were moving. On the horizon, the sun hung low but not quite setting yet, its rays glinting off the perfect turquoise waters. With a drink in hand and the breeze whispering over her skin, it would've been the perfect moment, if not for the frown on Javid's face as he contemplated his answer.

'It isn't unexpected that not everyone was thrilled about the choice for Riyaal's new ruler. There's been some…dissent.'

She sucked in a breath. 'Dissent? How much?'

'Nothing that won't be resolved eventually.'

'And yet it's serious enough for you to be taking calls on your honeymoon?'

A smile flashed before it disappeared. 'I may have been foolish in letting my advisors believe they have twenty-four-hour access to me. They're taking full advantage of it,' he said a touch ruefully.

The throb of worry didn't dissipate despite his answer. 'Who are the dissenters?'

'The head of the Al-Mejdi family. Adnan made him promises he didn't get around to keeping. And he believes he should've had a say in who Riyaal's next ruler should be.'

Anaïs remembered the late King had been prone to making lofty pledges in the heat of the moment, a flaw her late cousin had lamented over frequently. 'Let me guess, his own son?'

'Indeed.'

'So what are you going to do?'

Javid took his time to sip his drink, his throat moving in a hypnotic swallow. With his gaze on the horizon and the sun reflected in his eyes, it was almost enough to make her forget what they were talking about.

'Diplomacy. For now.'

'And if that doesn't work?'

He turned to her, his eyes gleaming. 'You doubt your husband's talents, *habibti*?' he rasped.

The endearment spiraled heat through her before settling low in her pelvis. She mirrored his movement and took a drink of her cocktail before answering. 'Isn't it best to always have a contingency plan?'

'*Na'am,*' he hummed. 'Mine tends to be harder negotiation. But I'm open to suggestions?'

'Making people like that feel important tends to make the problem go away. I know of the Al-

Mejdi family. There are three grown sons and two daughters. If the father is stalling negotiations, find out what the sons and daughters are good at and offer it to him without compromising our principles. Let them do the work of defusing the situation with their father.'

His eyes widened in surprise, then he smiled. 'I'll be the first to admit I'm wrong. Pandering to their egos might just win over diplomacy.'

Anaïs couldn't have stopped her responding smile if she'd tried. Nor could she stop the warm feeling swelling through her.

Javid's gaze lingered on her face for several seconds before dropping to her neck and throat.

She fought the urge to fidget as he conducted a slow appraisal of her body, then took a bold, precise step towards her. She was immediately assailed by his scent, by the exhilarating power of his nearness. Hell, even the simple act of lifting his glass to take another sip enthralled her.

'Enough shop talk. You look bewitching, *ma chérie*. Entirely captivating.'

'Thanks, but the sunset—the only captivating reason for our being here—is that way.' She jerked her head to the west.

'I'm aware,' he drawled without redirecting his gaze from her.

'You're straying towards cliché, Your Majesty.'

'But your blush tells me it's not entirely ineffective, *ma reine*,' he returned.

Anaïs feared in that moment that it would always be like this. He would torment and tease her, leaving her unsettled with each encounter. And her emotions would continue to wobble on that knife-edge, caught for ever between giddy nervousness and sexual stimulation.

How long could she sustain it without going insane?

'So much serious thinking,' he mused, his voice holding that same throb that echoed low in her pelvis. 'What's going through that clever brain, I wonder?'

'Strategising the next way to floor you, of course. What else?'

His smile was broader. And devastating. Her heart skipped several beats when he gave a low, guttural laugh that did indecent things to her insides.

She was still pleading with her body to pipe down when he lifted his hand and trailed his fingers just below where the emerald necklace rested.

'I so look forward to our next stimulating skirmish.'

By some silent signal, the staff had returned. One stood at the entrance to the half-covered part of the deck where their dinner table had been set up. Somewhere nearby soft music piped up from hidden speakers, setting the mood far too effectively.

As a scene for the first evening of a married

couple on their honeymoon, it was beyond exquisite. As a battleground for supremacy in their little game… Anaïs couldn't help but feel she was already on losing ground.

Once upon a time, this was everything she'd wished for herself.

Before betrayal.

Before heartache.

'I'm beginning to feel like I should be offended at that look on your face.' There was a bite to his voice that dragged her attention back to him.

'Not everything is about you, you know.'

That her answer didn't please him was evident in his flaring nostrils. 'In this time and place, I beg to differ. We're on our honeymoon. Everything should be about you and me only. No room for anyone else.'

Anaïs forced herself to take a breath. 'If you must know, I didn't think I'd be here under these circumstances,' she reluctantly confessed.

For a split second, he looked confused. Then his face tightened. 'Ah, you imagined being here with someone else. Your ex-fiancé, perhaps? You were engaged once, weren't you?'

Her gaze flew to his, her eyes widening before she remembered the report he'd mentioned. Confirmation that he knew about Pierre soured the food in her mouth.

'Should I have been so distasteful as to commission a report into your past love life too?'

He shrugged, that hard-edged look on his face not dissipating. For a wild moment, Anaïs wondered if that episode in the private restroom at their wedding, when he'd declared he didn't share in that, oh, so primitive and possessive way, was about to repeat itself. And then she wondered why the hell she wasn't offended by it. Why it sent a kick of sensation through her body.

'It wasn't driven by idle curiosity,' he finally answered.

'Then why—?'

'Do you keep in touch with him?' he pressed, ignoring her question.

Recalling his response to her own query about the presence of his past liaisons at their wedding, she swallowed. 'Not every relationship ends amicably,' she snapped, then regretted the little telling outburst.

His gleaming eyes told her she'd drawn his interest. 'What happened?'

'If I said I don't want to talk about it, would you simply override me and go digging?'

'No, but it would remain a mystery. And I don't like mysteries.'

The effortless arrogance with which he made the statement should've taken her breath away. Sparked outrage. And yet the simple truth that he was showing his character and not attempting to wear sheep's clothing over his wolfish nature took the edge off her ire.

'If you must know, he betrayed me in every way imaginable that a man can betray a woman. I discovered that he had no intentions of leaving his playboy ways behind him. Ever. I guess once a playboy always a playboy?' The question was pointed enough to garner a sharp-eyed look from him.

'I hope you haven't taken the foolish notion to tar us with the same brush?' he demanded icily.

'Are you offering that all playboys aren't cut from the same cloth?' she scoffed, even while a part of her wanted him to answer in the affirmative.

Why?

Because not finding similarities between Pierre and Javid crumbled her resistance? Because then she could hope that the kindred feeling she'd experienced when they'd talked about ruling together both in public and in private was sustainable?

If she'd expected a sardonic response, she was to be disappointed. If anything, Javid looked even more displeased, his eyes narrowing on her face.

'I've ensured that no woman is speaking with such disparaging censure about me anywhere in the world.'

'Are you sure?'

His lips tightened. 'No liaison of mine has ended with accusations of misleading or broken promises.'

'So it's their fault if their expectations get their hearts or feelings hurt along the way?'

The mocking smile made a fleeting return. 'You know better than to lure a diplomat into hypotheticals, *ma chérie*. What makes you think any of the women in my past had more than fleeting feelings for me?'

'Is that your way of evading the question?' she returned, a tiny dart of shock going through her at the thought that his liaisons had all been superficial. What woman in their right mind wouldn't want to…?

No! She was not going to finish that thought. That way lay extreme foolishness and danger.

'It's my way of telling you that if you wish to cling to the belief that I'm anything like the man who broke your trust, then you should ask yourself why.'

With that cryptic answer, he stepped close and caught her elbow.

Anaïs was busy grappling with the question when he escorted her to the table. Looking around, she saw that the yacht had made a slight course turn so that they weren't heading towards the horizon but sailing parallel to it. And that gave them an even wider view of the beginning of the breathtaking light show that was a Bora Bora sunset.

They were treated with the orange gold along with their first-course dish of grilled lobster and lemon and cream sauce, washed down with a sublime vintage white wine. Then the washes of mauve arrived, blending with the orange and gold and making Anaïs literally gasp out loud as the sky was filled with the vivid colour.

Caught in the spell of the moment, she glanced over at Javid to find him watching her, the same enigmatic but intense look on his face that spiralled a fizz of sensation through her.

The ambience of the evening had altered again. The edgy tension had disappeared once their first course was served, and he'd slipped into that sophisticated charm she'd seen him practise with the opposite sex frequently.

And she…?

She found herself wishing for that earlier connection when they'd been in harmony about Riyaal. Perhaps it was the champagne talking, but those moments had filled a longing she'd thought was buried for ever.

So when she found herself in Javid's arms after dinner, swaying to sultry French ballads crooned by her favourite songstresses, she didn't fight it.

He'd asked her to dance after dessert with that glint in his eyes, just when the whole sky had turned a deep, magnificent purple. And she'd refused to back down.

So when his arm tightened a fraction around her waist and he drew her close, she allowed her hand to rest at his nape, glorying in the slight tens-

ing in his body when she toyed with the strands
of hair resting there.

She told herself the synchronised beating of
their hearts was just biology, that what his lingering eyes on her mouth triggered inside her just
physical. And yet that craving didn't subside. That
notion that she wanted Javid over and above this
marriage of convenience was deeply unsettling.

He had suggested he wasn't a playboy like
Pierre. Something in her yearned for that to be
true.

An unsettling sensation snaked through her.
How far was she prepared to let this go to test
it? A touch? She was already doing that. A kiss?
More?

She swallowed.

'So much internal debate again, *habibti*?' he
mused, his movements utterly suave as he danced
her from one corner of the deck to the other. 'I'm
surprised you haven't worn yourself out.'

She allowed herself a small smile. 'Maybe I've
got more stamina than you imagine.'

Immediately his eyes darkened until his pu-
pils were swallowed within the blackness around
them. The effect was so dramatic, she gasped
softly.

His hands tightened a fraction more before releasing her. 'This is where I'm supposed to say I
look forward to testing it out and you accuse me
of spewing more cliches?'

Her surprise must have shown on her face because he gave a droll smile.

'Isn't it?' she dared.

'In some ways, perhaps. I'm a virile male with his beautiful wife in his arms, after all. But your stamina isn't a surprise to me. A lesser man would've been battered down by your resistance to this marriage.'

'I hear a double-edged compliment in there somewhere,' she responded.

A flash of a smile stole her breath, as many acts from him had tonight. 'Or perhaps I'm attempting to tell you we're both superior beings, who should claim what they want without all the chess moves.'

The serious edge to his tone made her tense. With nerves. With a thrilling sort of excitement that shouldn't have had a place in this skirmish. And yet it did. It made her hold her breath. Made her yearn for things she'd thought she'd abandoned years ago. Thankfully, it was the power of that yearning that made her regroup. Fast.

'Is this a double or triple bluff?' she flung at him, returning her hand to the safety of his jacket-clad shoulder.

Something close to disappointment flashed then stayed in his eyes, the slight downward turn of his lips searing her absurd alarm. Absurd because she should have zero qualms about disappointing him. And yet the feeling remained as they continued to sway.

But the atmosphere altered yet again, a cool distance wedging and stilting their conversation for the remainder of the evening.

And when he escorted her to their adjoining suites two hours later and bid her a cool goodnight, Anaïs told herself it was for the best. She'd spent an evening that could be classed as romantic with Javid Al-Riyaal and she hadn't succumbed to his charms.

She had to take that as a win.

So why then did she slide into bed with a hollowed ball of yearning in the pit of her stomach?

CHAPTER SEVEN

FOR THE THIRD day in a row, Javid found himself on his terrace at an ungodly hour.

He bit back a self-deprecating smile that cracked at the edges. His concentration was shot to pieces. Sure, he still managed to function enough to rule his kingdom from afar; even pull a few challenging diplomatic feats together without too much loss of face.

But beyond that, in the interminable hours that should've passed with sublime pleasure in paradise, he was facing an immovable fortress of resistance.

And the cause of it…

His wife.

He glanced at the firmly shut French doors only a handful of strides away across the terrace. Excruciatingly close yet so far away.

Like the woman herself.

For the past three days, she'd driven him half insane. On the one hand, she'd confirmed that he'd been justified to push for a conciliatory union. Her ideas on how to better rule Riyaal were nothing short of innovative. Her fears of not being good enough hadn't totally diminished but they'd receded enough for Javid to see she was beginning to settle into her new role.

Surprisingly, that increasingly eased his own misgivings about being King. For the first time in his life, he didn't feel so...solitary.

She also unfailingly spent enough time with him to satisfy the 'honeymoon' etiquette. When he caressed her cheek, she immediately reciprocated with a touch to his jaw or a hand on his arm. She returned his smiles with blinding ones that sucked the oxygen from his lungs.

Even her unfettered enjoyment of the island was bewitching. She explored the crystal-clear waters in skimpy bikinis that drew muted curses and blasted his libido with enough firepower to fuel a small kingdom.

But inevitably, she withdrew. Always.

Leaving him with a deepening craving that would've been amusing were it not so intensely maddening.

He had to hand it to her. She was establishing herself as the most unique woman he'd ever known.

But her continued rejection was also reopening old wounds, reminding him of his attempts to elicit a response from those who'd been content to leave him on his 'spare' shelf until he was needed to perform some duty or other. Like his parents…

Then, as now, the consequences had left him even more hollow, his efforts seeming to do nothing. Reach neither his mother nor his father.

Was he in danger of a repeat, albeit on a different level? Did harsher rejection and ultimately indifference await him on this unknown?

Chest tight, he diverted his gaze to the horizon. At least he hadn't missed a single spectacular sunrise since he'd been here.

Lifting his espresso cup to his lips to down the whole mouthful, he revelled in the scalding heat, hoping it would take his mind off his wife for one mocking minute.

The sound of the doors opening behind him put paid to that moment of respite. He knew the moment she saw him. Heard her soft gasp and the halt of her light footsteps.

'Oh, you're here.'

'Such a rousing response to my presence.' He tried, really tried, to resist looking her way. Of course, he failed within moments. He turned, his gut clenching at the sight she made. Even sleep-tousled she was breathtaking.

Or maybe he was just sex-deprived. Santa Barbara felt like a distant, unsatisfactory past, the faces of the women blurred beyond recognition.

Surprisingly, he didn't yearn for those days.

Even in the short time since he was crowned, the challenges of ruling had taken precedence over all else.

Well…*most* things.

'Is that coffee?' She changed direction and headed for the tray of coffee he'd had delivered half an hour after realising sleep was once again eluding him. 'Do you mind?' she asked.

He waved her on, unable to stop his gaze from following her delicious outline beneath the filmy layers of her nightgown and robe.

She poured her coffee with that simple but elegant movement that absurdly fascinated him so much. Then, to his surprise, she approached where he stood.

He warned himself he shouldn't be pleased, that she probably had more torment up her sleeve. But all she did was gaze at the horizon for a minute before turning to him, one hand dragging the thick sheaf of her hair over one shoulder.

'So what's the plan for today?' she said after she'd blown softly on her hot beverage…and sent a thousand more spears of lust into his groin.

His lips twisted as he stared into his empty cup. 'More torture, I expect.'

He felt more than saw her startled gaze. 'Pardon me?'

His nostrils flared as the soft breeze arrived with her warm, alluring scent on it. One hand gripping the stone wall to stop from reaching for her, from burying his face in that delectable curve of her neck and breathing her in, he managed a smile. 'You've snorkelled, waterskied and jet-skied, and parasailed. Sunbathed and explored most of the island. All while putting on a superb exhibition of affection for whoever's watching. So perhaps *you* tell *me* what's the plan for today?'

Her eyes narrowed and, again, he alarmingly felt a burst of anticipation at the possibility of tussling with her. 'If I didn't know better, I'd think you were griping about the very thing you wanted, Your Majesty.'

And there was the other thing. He was used to everyone being courteous to the point of obsequiousness around him. Not his wife. She used his title when she was riled and didn't give a damn about the consequences.

As for his griping...

A distance flash from the corner of his eye that could've been the gardener beginning his work or just a shadow of a tree was all the excuse he needed to tell himself to reach out and touch her. To drag an errant strand of hair over her ear and trail his fingers down the side of her neck.

Her decadent shiver at once soothed and energised him. And when she didn't move away, he stepped closer. 'Maybe I am,' he mused in a low tone. 'Maybe I've grown bored with this status quo and wish to change things up a bit.'

She took another gulp of coffee, her eyes narrowing on his as she swallowed. 'Change things... how?' she asked, wariness in her voice.

He wasn't going to admit he didn't know. Wasn't going to confess that he was floundering. What he was going to do was stop fighting this colossus of desire that was devouring him alive.

'Enough so I can get some damn sleep at night,' he growled, before he promptly relieved her of her coffee cup. He paused long enough to set it on the terrace wall before he dragged her into his arms.

Her gasp washed over his lips right before he smothered it between their kiss, then groaned when she opened up for him. It was hard and deep and brief enough to signal everything he wanted. Everything he planned on doing to her. And when he drew back as abruptly as he'd initiated the touch, he kept her in his arms, steadied her when she swayed.

'Touch me back,' he demanded, his voice a hoarse, needy mess. 'Please.'

Her hands fluttered at her side and he held his breath, but a moment later they stilled, resting against her hips. 'There's no one here to see.'

That echo of rejection from his parents caught him in its grip again. But he pushed it away. They were emotionally connected in their caring for Riyaal, in their bid to rule as a unit, but this was purely about the physical. This was about ridding himself of the insanity she'd somehow created within him. 'Then touch me because you want to.'

Her eyes widened, and again he caught that curious and tantalising glimpse of siren and innocent, yearning and abstention. 'Javid... I...we shouldn't...'

'On the contrary, we should do whatever we want. But don't convince *me*, Anaïs. Walk away if you manage to convince yourself that you don't want me. Then we'll both know the truth.'

Her nostrils fluttered in the most charming way, while her pink tongue drew out to flick over her bottom lip.

Javid smothered a groan and forced himself to remain still. To be patient despite the rampaging need to grab and devour. To taste again and take her until they were both too sated and exhausted to move a muscle.

Moments ticked by. Her lips parted as her breathing grew shallow, her beautiful eyes widening and darkening with the strength of her desire.

'Say it, Anaïs,' he pressed hoarsely when he knew he couldn't stand the torment for another second. 'Say it and give us both what we want.'

The shake of her head slammed something hard and desperate inside him. And Javid knew in that moment that he'd never wanted anything as much. Which was intensely disturbing to admit.

One taste of her would resolve all that, he sternly promised.

One taste and the insanity would abate.

'I don't think—'

'Maybe you shouldn't overthink it at all. Take what you want, *ma reine*. And don't apologise for it.'

He knew the moment the suggestion found fertile soil. Her gaze dropped from his to take in his bare torso, to sizzle over every inch of his skin so he felt as if he were on fire. Below his waistband, his already awakening shaft thickened, the glorious rush of blood making him dizzy.

She noticed her effect on him when her gaze dropped lower.

Her beautiful eyes widened even further, and it was all he could do not to throw her over his shoulder and carry her off. But he wasn't an alpha male with the vanquishing blood of his ancestors running through his veins for no reason. So he pressed his advantage by leaning close and running his tongue over that maddening pulse racing at her throat.

And when she whimpered but didn't push him away, he tasted her for longer, groaning at the feel of her silky skin beneath his tongue. 'Sweet heaven, but you taste glorious.'

A soft moan, and her hand found his shoulder,

her head tilting to grant him better access. But as much as he wanted to lay her on the stone terrace and pound into her, he forced himself back.

When her eyes found his, he exhaled. 'Say it, Anaïs,' he insisted.

Another slick of her tongue over her juicy lips. A deep breath. Then, 'I want you.'

'Enough to allow yourself to have me without reservation?' he pushed, because, while he could practise restraint with the best of them, he too had his breaking point. *Na'am*, the playboy prince, now King of Riyaal, could only last a mere three days at the hands of a temptress before he succumbed.

'Without reservation,' she assented, her voice sexily husky as she licked her lips once more.

'You're going to have to stop doing that.'

Her gaze flew to his. 'What?'

Javid bit back another groan, then, swooping low, he caught her lower lip between his teeth. 'That. Among other things.'

One eyebrow rose. 'You have other objections?'

'The way you've been driving me mad these past few days? I have a veritable laundry list, my sweet.'

Heat rose in her cheeks and this time his curse ripped free. Because it turned out his wife couldn't breathe without turning him on.

'I look forward to hearing them and proving that it's all your own fault somehow.'

He laughed, the sound and sensation curiously lightening something inside him. Before it could add to the conundrum, he swung her up in his arms, striding purposefully for his suite. 'Later. Much later, I think,' he said, and watched another wave of heat sweep over her face.

Had he not been holding her, he wouldn't have felt the tension whip through her body the moment he stepped into his bedroom. But he felt it, saw her gaze dart to the bed he'd rumpled with his restless night before skittering away.

As if she was nervous.

As if she was...untried?

Javid paused, his eyes narrowing on her face. Had her previous lovers really left her so unsatisfied that all this still seemed new enough to her?

On the one hand, the blaze of unfamiliar jealousy lighting through him made him irrational enough not to want to ask. On the other...

'Something you want to tell me, *ma femme*?' It felt good and, yes, primitive to call her that. If that made him a caveman...he shrugged inwardly. That too would be added to the mania that was his current state.

There was a determined boldness in the hand that curved around his neck, the face she raised to his, and the gaze that practically devoured his mouth in open invitation. 'You've shown me that we can be united in rule. I don't take this step lightly, Javid. Don't disappoint me.'

That clench in his gut came again. Another man would admit he was…moved by her statement. Awed by her trust. And yet, he couldn't shed the notion that she was holding something back from him.

He would find out soon enough, he promised himself, right before he reclaimed her lips and groaned at the sublime feel and taste of her. Her warm, pliant body seemed made for his arms, the mouth clinging to his moulded just for his. Perhaps he was delirious from so much wanting and he was spinning fantasies, but Anaïs felt…*right* in his arms. So much so that when the first series of trembles moved through him, he experienced that further unnerving that warned that he was skating on dangerous ground.

Then her fingers were tightening at the back of his neck, her nails sinking into his skin in that unique clutch caress that drove him insane, and he abandoned the path of his thoughts. Abandoned everything but drawing her tighter into his body until her softness was imprinted on his hardness, until her scent was the only thing he wanted to breathe in for evermore.

Until it was imperative that he walk her the last few steps to his bed and lower her onto it, drag the robe from her body and move his lips down the silky smoothness of her neck, her shoulder, the top of one plump breast.

Her breathing hitched even further when he trailed kisses over the mound, and when, with a deep groan, he tongued her nipple and sucked it into his mouth, she shuddered and gasped, it was the best sound in the entire universe.

Greedy for more of that sound, for more of her, he gripped the delicate material and tugged. The material ripped. She gasped again, and, fuelled by that same primitive instinct, he pushed away from her, kneeling over her as he ripped the entire garment in two.

Wide eyes flitted from the torn clothing to his face, her breathing even more erratic as they stared at one another.

'Tu es fou,' she gasped, but she licked her lips again, betraying her true feelings on his actions.

'Yes, I'm insane. You...' He leaned forward and palmed one breast in his hand, the feel of her near overwhelming him. 'You make me that way.'

At her delicious tremble, he fell on her, a ravenous creature he barely recognised who needed her more than he needed air.

He kissed his way down her body, intent on discovering every inch. Perhaps then he might uncover what it was about her that made him this way. But by the time he reached the silky curls crowning the apex of her thighs, by the time he inhaled her mouth-watering scent, he knew the hunger clawing through him wouldn't abate any time soon.

Perhaps even…

No. He wasn't going to entertain the dangerous possibility of continuity.

With renewed determination, he parted her thighs, teased his lips from inner thighs to knees and back again, until she was writhing with need, her own hunger mounting alongside his. Only then did he deliver the ultimate kiss, gliding his tongue over her soft flesh while she cried out in hesitant delight that made his instincts tweak once again about her experience before, again, he delved into the moment, his senses on fire as he pleasured her.

Javid had had many lovers, but none as spontaneously responsive as Anaïs. It was almost as if her own reactions were new to her, her gasps filled with startled surprise and delighted enthusiasm.

It was…unique. Stimulating. *Addictive.*

So he drew out her pleasure, until she was frantic. Then he delivered the coup de grâce, his own guttural groans echoing in the room as he revelled in her sublime climax.

Anaïs had thought that seeing Javid out on the terrace clad in only his pyjama bottoms with all that gorgeous bronzed skin on show was torture enough. She'd endured days of it, while trying to keep her emotional fortress from crumbling underneath the power of her yearning for *more*.

Watching him rise from the bed, still caught up and breathless in the aftermath of the most intense release of her life, was a different level of delightful torture entirely. He shed his clothing without a stitch of self-consciousness, an animalistic assurance about him that only heightened the charges of desire whipping in the room. She'd fooled herself into thinking she was sated from his divine pleasuring but at the sight of his naked, powerfully masculine and virile body, she knew she'd barely scratched the surface of her need. A need she now knew—despite having been limited to kisses and heavy petting—had been nowhere near this intense in her last relationship.

Frankly, this eye-opening experience made her thankful for her lucky escape from Pierre. Because if this was what had been in store for her all along...

Javid prowled onto the bed, the flex of his muscles mesmerising, and she willingly stepped away from the awful memories. But as he drew closer after sliding on contraception, the fever in his eyes echoing the one reignited in her blood, a different tension took hold of her.

She'd caught his occasional circumspect looks, knew she'd almost given herself away with her untested reactions to his touch.

Tell him...

Anaïs wasn't sure why she held her virgin status a close secret. He would discover it for himself soon enough, after all. She swallowed as his incredible body hovered over hers. Those eyes were probing hers again, the laser focus at once exhilarating and alarming. She'd known from their first meeting that she'd never met anyone as intense as Javid but, having been subjected to his presence in the last several days, Anaïs had been introduced to a whole new level of intensity. When she was with him, it was almost as if he had to absorb her every reaction, had to witness her every emotion. He watched her with single-minded focus that made her feel as if there wasn't a single other thing he was interested in in that moment. She'd never felt anything like it.

Wasn't sure she ever would.

Something sharp and fierce caught her unawares on the heels of that thought, making her heart hammer as they stared into each other's eyes.

'Spread your thighs for your husband, *mon soleil*,' he growled against her lips.

Another helpless shiver raced through her. The endearments that fell so effortlessly from his lips were yet another chink in her armour. That he knew uttering them affected her this way should have made her warier. Instead, it made her melt. Made her succumb to that flame-edged demand

and part her legs, made her watch his glance linger on the place he'd feasted on just a short while ago. Watch his nostrils flare and his cheekbones heat up with arousal as he positioned himself against her heated entrance and pinned her once more with his dark gaze.

'Now, eyes on me. Watch me take you, *habibti*.'

Every cell in her body charged to life at that command, every sense wide open as anticipation trapped the breath in her lungs. She opened her mouth then, probably to finally confess what awaited them both, but words failed her.

So she met his gaze, let herself be utterly consumed by the lustful pledge in his eyes as he thrust, true and deep, a dark growl falling from his lips as he buried himself inside her.

Only to still at her sharp cry.

Anaïs watched as, incrementally, shock froze his pleasure, his eyes widening as he took in her fleeting discomfort and the truth of her status rammed home.

'Anaïs?' His voice was ragged with disbelief. Uncertainty. Faint accusation.

Spying the last one, she started to lower her gaze.

Insistent fingers clenched in her hair. 'No. Look at me.'

She swallowed, the argument she'd deftly initiated internally withering away under his fiery gaze.

'Explain,' he breathed.

She attempted a shrug that only half lived before dying. 'It's… I've never…you know.'

His eyes flared, then narrowed. 'How can that be? I distinctly recall you taunting me with exes at our wedding in a bid to aggravate me.'

'Exes don't necessarily mean men I've slept with.'

His nostrils flared. 'Don't play semantics with me, Anaïs.'

Nerves dragged her tongue over her lips. He gave another growl and she felt him twitch inside her, the effect so delicious and new she tentatively chased after it with a tiny jerk of her hips.

His jaw clenched, the colour flaring anew on his cheekbones as his other hand clamped on one hip. 'There will be no pleasure until I have answers.'

'It's self-evident, isn't it?' she tossed out, growing a little desperate as need built in her pelvis. 'I never got around to sleeping with my fiancé. Or any other man, for that matter.'

'Never got around?' he echoed, disbelieving, then cast a look down her body. 'Either he's completely blind or—'

She shut him up the only way she could think of in that moment. By rearing up and sealing his lips with hers. And because she'd gained knowledge from their previous encounters, she slid her tongue across the seam of his mouth, felt him shudder before he groaned.

Taking that small triumph, she pulled back. 'Do

you really want to talk about this now?' she whispered against his lips. 'I thought men like you valued purity. Or is it the idea that you'll have to tutor me on how to please you that irritates you?' Pierre had vacillated between those opinions, which at the time had confounded her. Did Javid think that too?

A different look filmed his eyes as his gaze once again raked down her body. The transit was slower this time, every inch of progress reflecting a deeper, more primitive possession in his gaze. As if he was staking a claim. As if her status had birthed a different sensation within him.

'If that's the case, you needn't worry,' she added hastily, the thought of losing this feeling, of losing *him*, making her heart stutter.

The eyes that rose to meet hers shocked with their unabashed stamp of utter ownership. 'Oh? And why not?' Despite the tossed-out question, his voice was thicker with possession. She might not have mentioned it, but her virginity had made its mark on him.

'Haven't you noticed? I'm a fast learner.' She squeezed her internal muscles and revelled in his sharp intake of breath and the thick curse that fell from his lips. The clench of his jaw as he tried to retain control.

Going one better, she teased her fingers over her nipple, unfettered sensation powering it into stiff points that had him gaping, his attention rapt as he panted.

'Anaïs. We will talk about this later.' There was warning and a touch of helpless desire in there that fired up her blood further, awakening the sleeping siren whose existence she hadn't had a clue about until just now. 'You're a witch,' he accused, right before he swooped down and took that peak between his lips. A lick and a deep suckle and the tables were turned.

She whimpered. Her hips strained of their own accord, seeking his possession as she clutched his shoulders.

'Is there something you want, *ma belle sorcière*?' he taunted gruffly, remaining still as she squirmed.

'You know there is. *Je veux plus,*' she moaned, her nails biting into his shoulders.

He shuddered, his eyes turning almost black with the power of his arousal. 'You want more? Are you sure, *habibti*?'

'*Oui.*'

'Say my name. Beg me. Tell me why you deserve to have more of me.'

'*Tu es terrible!*' she cried, cringing a little inside at her plaintive, yearning tone.

He flicked his tongue lazily over one turgid nipple, then sucked it into his mouth for a few delicious pulls before he released it to answer. 'No, my dear. I'm not so terrible. I just want what I want and I'm greedy for you. Give it to me and you get yours.'

Her nails dug harder into his skin, and he knew he'd bear the marks—proudly.

'More, please, Javid. Give me more,' she breathed shakily.

His fingers massaged her scalp, his eyes drilling into hers, his expression so raw and demanding she felt as if she were being turned inside out. 'Again. But in French.'

Her eyes widened. 'Why?'

'Because I find it turns me on.'

She repeated it and commanded, then gasped as she felt him thicken even harder inside her. *'Oh, mon Dieu.'*

'Exactly. And now you've given me what I want…'

He gripped her nape to hold her steady and let action finish the rest of the sentence. Action that bowed her spine and she thrashed her head in wild abandon. Action that made her sob her pleasure as he drove repeatedly into her, lyrical Arabic words spilling in guttural waves from his lips, sending her into an even wilder frenzy, until she had no choice but to explode beneath the force of it. To scream his name even louder as sensation ripped her to a thousand tiny shreds.

Javid watched the most confounding woman he'd ever met writhe with pleasure beneath him and struggled to catch his breath. On the one hand he was pleased his instincts hadn't let him down. He'd caught glimpses of her innocence because she had been a true *ingénue*. Far more so than he'd accommodated for.

A *virgin.*

He squeezed his eyes shut as the word echoed through his brain, thickening his blood and other vital parts of him that had her gasping anew. As her tightness clamped harder around him and he was sure he would take complete leave of his senses within moments.

A handful of minutes ago he would've sworn he didn't care whether a woman he slept with was experienced or not. Discovering that his wife was completely untouched had shifted something within him, a possessiveness that seemed to expand with every thrust, with every gasp from her sweet lips and every helpless grunt from his chest. This gift she'd kept secret until she'd had no choice but to divulge its existence shouldn't move him profoundly. But Javid knew why it did.

It was the first truly unique thing he'd ever been given.

There was no second-hand indifference in this. There was no taking it back.

And even now, as he opened his eyes to find Anaïs staring up at him, willingly offering her body with a shy smile that grew bolder at glimpsing the power she had over him, he knew it would hold its place as one of the most earth-shaking experiences of his life.

Perhaps *the* most?

He dropped down and took her mouth again, reluctant to cement that thought. Because if he did then he was risking her holding an important place in his life.

Perhaps *the* most?

Another growl leapt from his chest, another primitive sound he couldn't seem to contain around this woman. What the hell was happening to him?

'Javid.'

Her shaken whisper of his name drove him over the edge he'd clung to for as long as possible. The last few thrusts lacked finesse and gentleness as his control finally snapped. As for the first time in his life, he lost all sense of time and place and became a desperate being of pure sensation, plastering her body to his as she cried out in climax and he followed, a willing slave to the endless bliss that consumed him.

In the hunt for his next breath, he couldn't summon the strength to push away the thought that something had changed here today. That as much as he was willing to still label this a control-wresting game and even a way to work his wife out of his system, it had definitely changed course. Just where it was taking him…them…he wasn't quite ready to contemplate yet.

So the moment he could breathe without his vision blurring, he rolled away. And found he wasn't quite ready to let her go. She was still plastered to him, her hand now resting on his chest. Hell, Javid didn't even mind her closed eyes. He could watch her in post-coital repose, her lips swollen from their frenzied kisses and her skin sheened in sweat they'd created between them.

Mine.

The single claiming word powered through him with the force that threatened to steal his breath again. Making him stiffen.

Making her eyes snap open, faint wariness in the gaze she raised to his.

Before he could question himself on that reaction or invite the same from her, he rose from the bed, plucked her into his arms and headed across the room.

'Where are we going?' she asked, one arm snaking around his neck.

God, how was it that she sounded even sexier? That hunger he'd slaked minutes ago was already rebuilding?

'I wasn't as…careful as I wanted to be. A warm bath should soothe you,' he replied, attempting to ignore what the combination of her blush and her smooth skin sliding against his did to his senses.

This would pass.

It had to.

But…perhaps not immediately?

'Thank you. But if that's why you look displeased, I'm fine.'

He slid her down to her feet when they reached the bathtub. Keeping one hand around her waist, he turned on the taps, tossed in scented bath gels before facing her. She looked more than fine. She looked utterly breathtaking.

'I'm not displeased.' He slid his fingers into her hair, delighting that she bared her neck when he tilted her head back. 'I'm…' Words failed him, then, and perhaps that was the first true inkling that this was unique enough to be dangerous to the distance and regimented control he'd put in place.

'You don't regret it?'

Her eyes were downcast, but her breath was held, as if awaiting a blow. And because he knew how that felt, he granted hasty reassurance.

'Absolutely not. And I'm attempting not to be a complete animal.' Not quite the accurate reflection but it was a part of the insanity, so he didn't take it back. Perhaps a little civility would help clear his head.

So he went one better and stepped away, disposed of the condom before lifting her into the water. And when he settled in behind her he busied himself shampooing her hair as the subject he'd pushed to the back of his mind surged forward, demanding attention.

'You don't owe me an explanation, of course, but I'd like to know why you didn't tell me you were a virgin, *habibti*.'

Anaïs had lost count of how many new emotions had pummelled her in the last hour of experiencing this series of *firsts*. At the very top, of course, was the sublime introduction to lovemaking—even though that felt like such a tame word for the tumult of losing her innocence to Javid Al-Riyaal.

And now, as she fought a losing battle against keeping her emotions under guard, she suspected the roller coaster was far from over. Because in this moment, she failed to imagine where else she would rather be. Who she'd rather be with than this man.

Perhaps it was a good thing her back was to him, although that was a small win since she was acutely aware of that firm column of manhood braced behind her. Was aware of the emotional excavation ahead of her.

'Anaïs.'

Question and command and warning. All wrapped up in the deep rumble of her name.

She sucked in a deep breath, not even bothering to regret that foolish taunt she'd thrown at him on her wedding day. 'Do you have something against a woman's right to choose who she sleeps with and when?'

His fingers stilled for a moment then continued his massage. 'If you're trying to throw me off by being offensive, it won't work. You know I don't.'

She bit her lip, grimacing with regret. 'I…didn't mean that,' she said in hushed apology.

'So?' he pushed.

'So…one way or another, circumstances prevented me from going through with the act.' Until now.

He didn't say anything, simply wreaked magic with his touch until her very spine felt as if it would melt into a puddle, melting the hold on her tongue right along with it. 'If you must know, casual sex never appealed to me.'

'There's baggage behind that statement,' he said, and there was no question. Only certainty.

She bowed her head, as if she could hide from it. His fingers slid to her neck, massaging her shoulders. Closing her eyes didn't stop the memories. Hell, it did the opposite. So prying her eyes open, she stared at the tiny kaleidoscope of colours displayed in the bath bubbles.

'My mother had a…few boyfriends when I was growing up. She seemed to require their affection with a frequency that…' She stopped, pressed her lips together.

'A frequency that was unconventional enough to trouble you?' he supplied, his voice oddly inflected.

'*Oui*. The older I got, the more a few of them seemed to think that I was automatically the same way. That I might welcome their attention.' Her voice had hushed, the memories dragging pain through her.

Javid exhaled a muted curse. 'Did any of them try—?'

'No,' she hurried to interrupt. 'I've heard of stories where that sort of attention wrecked families, but Maman was never angry with me. But she would break it off if any of them tried anything. And then immediately try to find a replacement.' A situation that had puzzled and hurt her long before she'd grasped that normal relationships between men and women weren't supposed to be like that. Then had come the deeper hurt of always coming second in her mother's rabid quest to find affection and acceptance elsewhere. Dauphine Dupont had pursued companionship as if she needed it to breathe, then finding fault in whatever current relationship she was in. Including the one with her own daughter. The serious fractures in their relationship had appeared when her mother had started suggesting that Anaïs wouldn't feel whole unless she followed Dauphine's example and found herself a man, too.

'It drove you to be the opposite. You solidified your façade as an ice princess to keep such men at bay. Effectively, I expect?'

She startled a little at Javid's intuitive response, so deep was she in past, troubling memories. 'I just couldn't see myself being...that way. Our relationship suffered when I wouldn't take her advice to find myself a man. She thought I was claiming to be better than her when I didn't base my self-worth on whether or not I was in a relationship. Or use my sexuality to secure a place for myself in a man's life.'

'But your views changed along the way, enough for you to get engaged?' There was an edgy note in his voice and on any other man, she would've labelled it jealousy. But Javid was a king, with every whim and desire there for his taking. Whim and desire that today had included her. A woman who'd served herself up on a silver platter.

Dismissing that jealousy as wishful thinking, she took another breath. 'I thought Pierre was different. He led me to believe he was.'

'Not very much gets past you, so I'm interested to know how he did that,' Javid mused, the edge still very much evident in his tone.

'By convincing me he was a reformed playboy,' she said, bitterness lacing her voice. Curiously though, it didn't weigh her down as much as it had only a few days ago. Anaïs shied away from the reason behind it.

'It obviously didn't work since you remained

untouched.' Was that smug satisfaction in his tone or was her discernment totally out of whack?

She stiffened. 'Are you pleased that his subterfuge didn't work or that he wasn't as brilliant a playboy as you?'

This time he exhaled harshly, and she didn't need to glance at him to know he was displeased. 'I believe we've established that I don't take favourably to being compared to any other male, *habibti.*'

'Have we?' she threw back, that persistent urge to rile him as she was riled resurging.

'Tell me what he did to make you so wish to punish all men.'

'Not all men. Just ones that believe there should be one rule for them and another for women.'

'Anaïs…'

What did it say about her that the rumble of her name sent frissons of excitement dancing through her? 'We worked together, which was probably not a great basis for a relationship when he was effectively my boss. We started going out a few months after he joined the company. He didn't call me frigid when I didn't sleep with him after the apparently requisite number of dates, which was… refreshing, I guess.' Especially after she'd gained an unfair reputation among her social group for rebuffing male attention.

'He was playing the long game.' The bite had

returned in Javid's voice, and once again a fool-ishly pleased sensation lit her blood.

She forced a shrug to dispel it but it lingered. 'Yes.'

'Why?'

'I never bothered to find out. It didn't matter in the end. All I know is that when I called him out on it, he made it seem as if I was at fault for not accepting it all along. That my little game of holding out had been amusing to him for a while but that I had to get real.'

'And getting real included…?' His voice was now an icy landscape, despite the still-soothing rotations of his massage.

'Telling me that he still wanted to marry me be-cause I was the kind of woman men like him mar-ried for respectability, but that, regardless of that, I shouldn't expect him to change. Then he went one better and gave me permission to indulge in the same open relationship he intended to pursue once we were married.'

This time Javid's curse was thick and fluent, with pithy French words thrown in there that drew hot blushes to her cheeks.

'You don't need me to remind you that you're a queen now. With many tools in your arsenal to make him regret the error of his ways.'

And what did it say about her feminist ideals that the bloodthirsty and predatory intent be-hind those words made flames light up inside her? That despite the bruising memories, even as she glanced over her shoulder at him, a reluctant smile twitched at her lips at his obvious fury on her behalf?

'I hope you're not suggesting I use my position to exact retribution? Because that would be frowned upon.'

'Hmm,' was all he rumbled, sending another shower of fireworks through her. 'I'm not *not* saying that, *ma reine.*'

My queen.

The reminder of her status sent another shiver through her, this one infused with power and responsibility. With the fact that now they'd consummated their marriage they were officially King and Queen.

Together.

But for how long?

The question came out of nowhere, knocking her several steps back. But before she could dig into this, Javid tugged her head back and kissed her long and deep.

'Wh-what was that for?' she asked in a daze when he lifted his head.

'Because you didn't relay any of that story in French,' he said.

'I...what?'

'I've discovered that you charmingly revert to your mother tongue when you're caught in emotion.'

Shock pulsed through her. *Mon Dieu*, just how much of herself had she given away with that? 'So you think that means it doesn't sting any less?' she asked, brazening her way out of the panicked realisation.

'Perhaps it stings but maybe not as much as you imagined it would. Deep inside you realise you've had a lucky escape, from the unwanted attentions of your mother's paramours and from your ex.'

Her panic escalated. Javid could read her emotions far too accurately. 'I thought you were a diplomat, not an amateur psychologist.'

His smile was twisted, laced with bitterness she recognised. 'Some symptoms are easy to diagnose when there's experience behind it.'

'You?'

His eyes darkened, began to shutter. *'Na'am.* But that's not a story for today. The water is getting cold.'

With that, he grabbed the nozzle and aimed it at her thoroughly shampooed hair. Briskly and efficiently, he changed over the water, then drew her back against his chest. 'Relax,' he rasped in her ear. 'For now, we'll let the past remain in the past.'

She held herself rigid for another handful of moments, then, because she was just as eager to let the unwanted memories recede, she sagged back against him.

Just as he continued. 'But now I understand you better, know that the challenge of making myself even more distinct is greater. So prepare yourself, *ma chérie.*'

CHAPTER EIGHT

DESPITE THE WARNING, Anaïs was still left repeatedly slack-jawed in the days that followed.

Many times she told herself she was foolish to take him at his word. But soon enough she discovered that Javid's every word or act was matched with evidence that attested to his true intent.

He dazzled her with brilliant conversation and charmed her with his dry wit. He increasingly sought her opinion in state matters when, regardless of his vows to enjoy his honeymoon, the challenge of being ruler encroached on their time.

Together they debated the merits of bringing forward the Riyaali World Expo—the global exhibition showcasing the best cultural talents and resources from around the world—that his late cousin had lobbied hard for, only to then slide it onto the back burner, because, like most things, Adnan had found the implementation more challenging than the idea.

Anaïs's enthusiasm about the project drew musing smiles from Javid. And when she dared him to let her form the committee to handle the PR for the whole event, she was stunned when he agreed.

That was the start of the revelation of what propelled the man she'd married. Every act was given one hundred per cent of his attention.

And when that attention was focused on her in the bedroom…

Her husband was insatiable for her, and she had absolutely no problem with it. And as day tumbled into night into new days, she accepted that she had less and less of a problem with his character as a whole. Hell, her opinion of him had refracted in the opposite direction, and now in her quiet moments Anaïs berated herself for how much she'd let her mother's unsavoury lovers and Pierre's treatment of her blight her vision.

Javid had never portrayed himself as something he was not. And as she saw him deal with his Riyaal matters and subjects, even from afar, her instincts pushed to accept him at his word.

As for sharing his bed…

Their intense compatibility had stunned her. Enough for her to drop her guard and contemplate where the harm was in doing so for as long as they were together.

As long as…

Three words that shot pangs of disquiet through her with increasing frequency.

'I've only been gone barely ten minutes and I've lost your attention. It doesn't please me.'

Anaïs kept her eyes shut behind her sunglasses, even as her stomach clenched at the deep, throaty voice, her senses happily screeching to life as Javid lifted her arm and trailed kisses from wrist to inner elbow.

'Being King doesn't grant you automatic monopoly on my time.'

'It should. I'm sure it's written into the constitution, somewhere.' Amusement laced the words, which in turn drew a smile to her lips.

'If it was, I'm sure you'd have highlighted it in neon by now.'

She felt him surge closer, his hand abandoning her arm to glide over her stomach and up to snag her waist.

Anaïs didn't need to turn to see him to know he'd reposed in that leonine way of his, his swimming-trunks-clad body stretching out next to hers on the double-wide lounger.

'I wasn't expecting you back for a while. The call sounded serious.'

'It was. Negotiations have stalled again with the Al-Mejdi family. The oldest son is standing with his father and encouraging his siblings to refuse our offer.'

Unease teased fresh alarm through her. It wasn't just because of the subject of the call. It was also because she felt guilty because she didn't want Javid's attention taken away from her. Nor did she want this honeymoon to be over. Yet.

To counteract that feeling, she forced her eyes open. Saw that his amusement had evaporated, his eyes narrowing on the middle distance. 'What's wrong?'

His hand continued to rove over her, ending up cupping one hip. Despite his touch, Anaïs could sense his troubled thoughts on the subject. 'As much as it grates, I fear we're coming to a cross-roads on this.'

'Que puis-je faire?' What can I do?

His gaze dropped to her, and one corner of his mouth quirking alerted her that she'd asked the question in French. She'd long given up guarding that part of herself from him. If it proved that she cared about what went on in Riyaal and about her people... She shrugged mentally. It was a state she didn't mind him knowing.

'You're already doing it, *habibti*. As for our problem, when outlandish demands are being made without concrete proof, it might be time for the law to handle it.'

'With investigations?'

'I might not have a choice. Riyaal won't be pushed into compromising its integrity in the eyes of its citizens or the world.' His tone was sombre but resolute.

Unable to resist touching to offer her support, she lifted a hand to his jaw. 'Do we need to return?' Every cell in her body rejected leaving this bubble but, still, she accepted the reality.

He hesitated then, his lips unerringly finding the centre of her palm and dropping a stomach-flipping kiss on her erogenous zone. 'We will play it by ear. I've given them a week to consider my latest offer. You and I will use that time to strategise further.'

Anaïs had no defence against the warmth and belonging that swelled in her heart.

Nor did she resist when he plucked her sunglasses off and tossed them onto the table nearby, then took her lips in a long, deep kiss, leaving her breathless when he lifted his head. Whatever he saw on her face drew a smug smile from him while one hand trailed up to cup her breast, toying with her nipple as he stared at her. 'I believe we have a midnight swim in a cove nearby minus our suits?' The thick husk of arousal told her just how much he was looking forward to that.

And because she'd already given herself away with the helpless writhing of her body, she curled her hand over his nape and dragged him down for another kiss. 'I can't wait.'

Ten hours later, Anaïs was thankful they'd been granted the idyllic midnight swim and picnic under moonlight. Because shortly after that, another phone call had shattered what was left of their honeymoon.

The Al-Mejdi family had brought their grievances to the world media and turned the delicate situation into a PR nightmare.

Javid's council advised his immediate return to Riyaal, which was how she found herself ensconced on the royal jet speeding back to the kingdom.

While Javid had been occupied on the phone from the moment they'd boarded four hours ago, Anaïs prudently familiarised herself with her upcoming duties. Javid used the larger conference room, while she used the desk in the master suite to conference-call with Faiza.

The young woman looked and sounded as meticulous as ever, but Anaïs didn't miss the strained expression on her face. 'Is everything all right?'

'Things have been a little tense, Your Majesty. But we're all hopeful now you and the King are on your way home.'

Anaïs frowned, biting her inner lip as guilt assailed her. Had she been selfish in enjoying her island idyll for this long when she was needed back home?

'I'm afraid with news of your role in the World Expo, your schedule is filling up rapidly, Your Majesty. Shall we go through it?'

She nodded, pushed the worry to the back of her mind, and started what turned out to be one of many long meetings ushering her into her role as Queen of Riyaal.

Some five weeks later, Anaïs looked back on

that baptism of fire as the mere tip of the iceberg. Weeks where she re-honed her PR skills while accepting that royal protocol was very much a way of her new life and learned how to delicately balance the two without causing a domestic or international incident.

It was also a period when she barely saw her husband. She'd put up a token argument when Javid had insisted she move into his suite on the night of the arrival. They'd celebrated her eventual capitulation by making furious love, then falling into bed only for Anaïs to wake up alone.

That had set the tone for the next several weeks. On the nights when he made it to bed, he would wake her with his hands and mouth, and she would eagerly fall into his arms, only to find herself alone again come morning.

On one pathetic attempt to gain his attention amid another bout of guilt for taking up his time when he was clearly needed by his people, she'd arrived in his office at a shockingly early hour, hoping to have breakfast with him.

His smile had been strained and distant, but he'd thankfully not sent her away. And yet, the meal had been strained, their conversation stilted when he wasn't tapping away at the tablet that had pinged repeatedly at his elbow or issuing instructions in Arabic to his hovering aide.

Anaïs had cut her losses soon after that and didn't attempt to monopolise his time again. Telling herself the pressures of ruling would ease didn't help the gulf she could feel building between them that had nothing to do with them being seated at opposite ends of the table at the handful of state banquets and hosting ceremonies they were required to attend. Especially when she'd witnessed first-hand during their honeymoon how utterly zealous he could be with his attention.

Accepting he wasn't zealous about *her* any more, that perhaps the honeymoon truly was over in every sense of the idiom, wedged a large stone in her chest, one that had grown every time she'd opened her eyes in the morning and seen, with more frequency, that he'd never been to bed at all.

When the ache continued to expand, the reminders of how things had been between them on the island bombarding most of her waking moments, she berated herself for being weak. For not being able to overcome the traits that had made her mother yearn for the validation of a man to make her feel whole. She was better than this, she self-admonished. She'd functioned adequately before Javid had stormed in and commanded every inch of her attention. She was a queen, *pour l'amour de Dieu*!

So why did her eyes prickle with tears and her heart ache with loneliness when she had mountains of meetings and Expo locations to tour with her all-woman committee this afternoon? When her life was so much more fulfilled than she would've admitted she'd enjoyed only a month or so ago?

After a quick glance and a sharp pang upon seeing that Javid's side of the bed hadn't been slept in, again, she rose from bed before Faiza could stride in and mother-hen her into action.

Then she paused as the strength leached momentarily from her knees. Sagging back to the bed, she shook her head to clear the fog and to swallow the curious surge of saliva in her mouth.

A minute later, once the haze passed, she headed across the room. Although she shared Javid's bed, she hadn't fully vacated the Queen's suite, and continued to use the opulent dressing room and bathroom.

Once showered, she shrugged on a flowing silk robe and was belting it on her return to have her breakfast meeting on Javid's private terrace when she screeched to a halt at the sight of her husband.

It'd been a while since she'd seen him clad in nothing but a towel, with rivulets of water from his recent shower still dripping over his chest and hard-packed stomach.

A different weakness assailed her as she stared. And stared.

'*Oh, je ne savais pas*— I didn't know you were in here.'

A look flashed in his eyes as he raked his fingers through his sodden hair. Anaïs thought she glimpsed an echo of her hunger, but it was gone almost instantaneously. 'I'm not stopping. I have a meeting in ten minutes.'

Despite the brisk, cool words he remained where he stood, his gaze raking her face before lowering to her chest. Her nipples puckered under his regard, and it was all she could do not to beg him to show her that the connection they'd shared on the island had been true. That this inability to shut him from her thoughts and her emotions, this...*upheaval* wasn't a one-sided thing. Her fingers tangled in her belt, her chest heaving as they stared at one another.

Then, as if tugged by an invisible cord, they surged towards one another.

His fingers tangled in her hair, one broad thumb tilting her face to his.

Her hands clung to his trim waist, and her lips parted.

The bedside phone rang.

A knock came at the door.

Just as suddenly as they'd come together, they sprang apart.

His lips thinned, the fire in his eyes cooling.

'Javid.'

He paused, then swung around, one eyebrow raised in response.

Anaïs licked her lips. *I miss you. We need to talk. What is happening?*

All weighted words that couldn't be set free for

fear it would release a seismic torrent of baggage she wasn't sure she wanted to deal with. So she fell back on the tangible. On the outer connection they'd both committed to.

'I'm touring a site for the Expo today. Your aide didn't confirm whether you could make it or not.'

The knock came again. Firmer. As Javid shook his head. 'I can't. But I look forward to your report. Have your office email it to me when it's done,' he said. Then walked away.

On legs that felt as weak as when she'd awakened, she opened the door to the butler, who announced Faiza's arrival. Her thoughts shattered by the definitive distance she couldn't ignore between her and Javid, she barely made it through the meeting. Was relieved when it ended. 'I'll be ready to leave for the site visit in half an hour.'

'But…didn't you hear what I said, Your Majesty?' Faiza asked, her face creased in a faint frown.

She rubbed at the faint throbbing at her temple. '*Excuses-moi*, what did you say?'

'There's a sandstorm approaching. We need to postpose the visit to tomorrow. Maybe the day after.'

'Oh. Okay. What's next on my agenda, then?'

Faiza stared down at the clipboard then glanced up contemplatively at Anaïs. 'Nothing that can't wait until the scheduled slot. You take the morning and early afternoon off if you wish, Your Majesty?'

Anaïs opened her mouth to say that was impossible…just as another wavelet of dizziness hit her. She'd been going full pelt for over a month, even filling her weekends because it was better than staying in the palace, pining for Javid. The idea of a whole morning off sounded like bliss. So, she nodded. 'That sounds great, *merci.*'

Faiza smiled. 'I'll let the butler know to bring you breakfast and make sure you're not disturbed. Unless you'd like the royal masseuse to attend to you?'

'No, thanks. I'm going to relax with a book and a possible swim later.'

Except neither of those plans came to fruition. The moment the butler entered the living room with her tray of breakfast, the smell of smoked salmon sent her bolting for the bathroom, the tea she'd drunk with Faiza exiting her stomach with enough force to make her sag weakly against the marble bathroom wall.

She was still there on her fifth vomiting bout when the palace doctor arrived half an hour later, discreetly summoned by the butler.

But by then, Anaïs didn't need to be examined to know her diagnosis.

Somewhere around the third bout of vomiting, suspicion had had her furiously working out her cycle, her jaw sagging when the truth exploded in her face. She was late by almost three weeks.

So when the female doctor entered the bathroom and saw the pregnancy test Anaïs had discovered—thanks to the bounty of the top-notch medicine cabinet tucked into one marble wall—she immediately helped Anaïs back into bed, and ordered her butler to bring her another tray of tea and dry crackers.

Once they were alone, the doctor smiled. 'Congratulations, Your Majesty,' she said, her professionalism slipping as her eyes sparkled with excitement and her smile went a mile wide. 'It would be my pleasure to assist you through this wonderful period.'

'I… *Oui, merci*,' she murmured, before shaking her head. 'I mean, thank you.'

'Of course, it won't always be smooth sailing. You'll need to start a course of vitamins. And the morning sickness will continue for…'

Anaïs barely followed the stream of instructions that followed, her mind spinning at the impact of the news. Pregnant. She was *pregnant*. Beneath the tray, she touched her flat stomach, awe spreading over her senses.

She was going to be a mother.

Javid was going to be a father.

The husband who'd barely spoken to her in a month. Who'd walked away from her this morning because he had better things to do than talk to his wife.

She was contemplating how she was going to break the news to him when the doors burst open and the man himself strode in.

Leonine eyes ablaze with ferocious fire latched onto her, then narrowed at the presence of the doctor, who was dipping in a reverent curtsy, before he launched across the room, that single-minded attention she'd so missed back in full force.

Could she trust it, though, when he'd switched it off so effectively the moment they'd returned to Riyaal?

'What's wrong?' he growled when he reached her, grasping both her hands in his.

A tremble seized her at his touch, her new reality subsumed by the fact that Javid would have this impact on her for ever. He would walk into a room, look at her, and she would forget about everything and everyone but him. Then she would search his expression, wonder which feelings were for her, and which were for himself and his duty and his people.

How quickly he would switch his focus and forget about her.

'I… Nothing—'

'*Nothing* doesn't make you throw up for an hour,' he grated. Swivelling his head, he pinned his gaze on the doctor.

The doctor opened her mouth, then, glancing

at Anaïs's stricken expression, she curtsied again. 'I think Her Majesty is best placed to deliver the news, Your Majesty. With your permission, I'll leave you two to it. I'll be close by if you need me.'

Javid tensed, then gave a brisk nod dismissing the doctor before turning back to her. 'Anaïs?'

She barely heard the doors closing. She drew her hands away so she could think straight without his magnetic effect scattering her thoughts. Displeasure flashed through his eyes, but he didn't reach for her again. Which absurdly tightened the vice in her chest.

As much as she yearned to attribute her jumbled emotions to pregnancy hormones, she knew it was far too convenient. Far too dangerous to shield herself from it. Best to face it now before she was blindsided. Again.

'Tell me what's going on,' he urged tightly, his brows clamped in a frown as he jerked to his feet and started to pace. 'If it's food poisoning, we'll need to have the kitchens thoroughly—'

'It's not food poisoning,' she interjected firmly, clasping her hands together to retain a modicum of composure. Then she forced her head up, met his gaze. 'It's morning sickness. I'm pregnant.'

The blood drained from his face. His jaw sagged in disbelief. Then shock skittered across his face. Widened eyes dropped to where the tray rested against her belly.

All emotions she'd experienced.

But it was the furious head-shake that sent cold shivers down her spine. The total rejection making her heart twist, then lurch in her chest.

'What? You…can't be,' he rasped, eyes turned burnished gold dull with shock.

'And yet I am,' she returned, thankful her voice remained steady despite the dreadful sensation sinking into her bones. 'We took precautions with contraception. But the reality is what it is.'

One hand cupped his nape in a harsh grip before reversing direction south to wedge in his pocket. His nostrils thinned as he inhaled harshly. 'How far along are you?' he bit out as he paced several steps away.

Her fingers shook as she stared at him, then realised she was searching his face for something… anything other than the biting chill of his interrogation. What she saw made her heart clench further. It was a look she recognised.

Distance. Wrapped in a suit of rejection. She'd seen it repeatedly on Maman, from the dates who'd labelled her frigid before she'd walked away from them. From Pierre.

Swallowing against the knot of despair in her throat, she answered. 'I haven't had a chance to fully work it out yet but it could be six weeks.'

His Adam's apple moved and, for the first time, Anaïs saw Javid less than one hundred per cent sure of himself. He was unnerved. And what did it say about her emotional state that even that fleeting glimpse of vulnerability made her yearn for him all the more?

For the longest time, his gaze rested on her. But he didn't approach. Didn't smile. Didn't reassure her that they were in this together. If anything, his features grew even more austere and when he moved it was farther away, to the French windows that overlooked their private courtyard.

Then she remembered what he'd said that evening before they were married.

Children are not part of my immediate future plans...

The cold words clanged in her head, sealing her misery.

Silence thickened between them until she was certain her nerves would shred irreparably.

'What happens now?' she blurted when she couldn't stand it any longer.

He turned. A muscle ticced in his jaw. Then his features neutralised. 'The only course of action available to us. We arrange for a doctor to perform a more thorough exam. We wait the appropriate time. And we announce the impending birth of our child to the kingdom and the world.'

The cold delivery of his words sounded the death knell to hopes she hadn't even allowed herself to admit she harboured until just now. Hopes, she realised, she'd started nursing during those heady days in the South Pacific. She'd fooled herself into thinking his single-minded attention could be something to build on, that their compatibility was a sound basis for a marriage.

How foolish and wrong she'd been!

'Then I guess there's nothing more to discuss right now.' Her voice held the barest quiver and she prayed he wouldn't hear it, even as she prayed he would refute her words, would stride back to the bed and *show* her how he felt about their news.

But he remained a stiff, imposing pillar at the far side of the room, his breathing steady and his form shrieking *His Majesty* as he watched her for an age. 'Do you have everything you need?' he demanded eventually; his tone coolly neutral.

Non, she wanted to shriek. 'Yes,' she replied instead. If nothing else, she would keep her dignity. Wouldn't beg for scraps of his attention as she'd done with her mother for years. If their time on the island was truly an aberration, then she was better off getting some distance from it too.

Even though she feared it was already too late. That Javid had woven himself into the fabric of her life in that way she'd been terrified of falling prey to her entire life. The way that whispered that her very happiness was wholly and unequivocally entwined with his. That while she could go through this life completely self-contained and fulfilled and *safe*, that fulfilment would be infinitely more precious if *he* were a part of it.

Were she to take the *risk*.

A curt nod, then, pivoting with artistic grace, he strode out of the room.

Anaïs collapsed against the pillows, a full-body tremble seizing her.

She'd been dancing around the truth for weeks now. But as the doors shut behind Javid, she finally accepted the reality. They might now be connected by this unbreakable bond of a child they'd created, but their connection on the island had been a dream, a wish she'd stupidly clung onto and dared to hope she could build on.

No more.

Her duties as mother and Queen were the only solid realities in her life now. And as her hand slid back over her stomach, she made a vow to do things differently. From her mother. From her husband.

For the sake of her child.

And as the sandstorm arrived and raged for the next two days, she made new plans. She moved from Javid's suite back to her own. And she attempted to barricade the heart that had come dangerously close to slipping into the grasp of someone else who didn't want it.

Forget world-altering threats of war, famine or calamities.

Javid was certain nothing had shaken him to his core like the announcement from his wife that she was carrying his child. Which in hindsight was laughable considering how much sex they'd had in the last few weeks. And how, with each bout of lovemaking, he'd grown even more desperate at the depth of his hunger for her. With the need to cling to that connection he'd never found with anyone else.

That gradual slide into dependency…hell, into *obsession*, wasn't an experience he'd relished.

It was why he'd latched onto the very valid excuse of the Al-Mejdi issue to keep his distance. He'd never experienced anything like it.

And yes, it unnerved him to the point of avoidance. To the point where he couldn't even have breakfast with Anaïs without craving her beyond madness. Couldn't see her beautiful body soft and breathtaking in sleep in his bed without the need to wake her and slake this infernal craving that had taken hold in his blood.

But…

A child. An heir. A lifelong responsibility that required more than diplomacy. That required… emotion. The kind he'd been deprived of during his formative years and therefore had no template to pass on to his own offspring.

He'd meant it when he'd said children weren't part of his future plans. Because the very idea filled him with dread. With the inescapable truth that he was ill-equipped to assume that role. And, more than the daunting role of King, this…sacred role…scared the hell out of him.

And two days after that bombshell had been dropped into his lap, he still shuddered with dread. Could barely take it all in. A new day had broken with him still pacing his office, where he'd spent yet another night—after being dealt another shock when he'd returned to his residence to find that Anaïs had relocated to her own—the enormity of what awaited him in the future weighing on his shoulders.

His gaze lingered on the phone on his desk.

His mother had attempted to reach out ever since Tahir had married and had a child of his own. Javid had spurned those overtures because there was nothing to salvage, in his opinion. Too little too late. She hadn't merely stood by while his father had treated him as if he was surplus to requirements, she'd actively distanced herself from him, too, sparingly offering attention only when it was required of her.

Lips pursing, he swivelled away from his desk. As much as he wanted an outlet for the chaos churning inside him, how could he rely on the mother who'd played a part in his alienation? Could he even trust whatever she wanted to say? His mouth dried at the thought of doing this alone, his stomach re-clenching in dread.

It was that same dread that had taken hold of him, preventing him from uttering anything that remotely hinted at the havoc coursing through him. Anaïs didn't need that. He couldn't visit his uncertainties on her.

With quick strides, he crossed to his desk, snapped up the phone and punched in the familiar number. His long inhale did nothing to calm him as he listened to the ringing echo.

'In case the clocks don't work in Riyaal, it's the crack of dawn,' his brother grumbled. In the background, Javid heard murmured words, then Tahir sighed. 'My wife tells me to be nice. So speak quickly, so I can be done and return to her arms.'

Javid grimaced, partly out of the lancing jealousy and partly because he'd rather not imagine his brother in that way, even though he would give much to be in the same position with Anaïs.

'Is this a silence contest?' Tahir mock growled, then he went quiet before rasping urgently, 'What's happened, brother?'

'My wife is pregnant,' Javid blurted before he could stop himself. He barely registered staggering backwards and collapsing into his chair, his free hand clawing through his hair.

Silence. Then, 'Ah. I take it, then, that you got over your threats to dismember me for suggesting you marry her? It's quicker than I expected but no matter—'

'Tahir,' he warned.

His brother sobered. 'I was in your shoes too, not so long ago, brother. It's…world-defining.' The thick emotion in his brother's voice made him wonder if he'd made a mistake calling him. Javid needed no-nonsense advice, not a man who was besotted with his new wife and son.

'I don't need colourful superlatives, Tahir. I need...' What did he need? Someone to grant him blanket assurances?

He heard more movement and sensed his brother had got out of bed. 'You want me to tell you you'll take to fatherhood like a duck to water?' Tahir stated in grave tones, that uncanny intuition that made him an exemplary ruler emerging. 'That our past baggage won't get in the way? I won't do you the dishonour of lying to you. It's a challenge you face with the mother of your child.'

Javid considered the strained relationship with said mother and pinched the bridge of his nose. 'You suggest a togetherness that's...lacking.'

'Then I suggest you do something about it. This is not the time for ambivalence, brother. This is the time to tell her what you want, but, more importantly, listen to what *she* needs.'

What if that isn't me? What if the strong woman I married has no use for me? What if I'm not enough?

Past insecurities shook through him as those words seeped like poison into his blood.

He swallowed, cobbled together the appropriate responses for his brother, then hung up minutes later with his mind still churning.

But as the sun rose and soared over his kingdom, Tahir's words ricocheted through his mind.

Tell her what you want, but, more importantly, listen to what she *needs.*

So what if his every need had been denied him as the second son and spare? So what if the doors to his emotions felt as if they'd rusted shut until very recently, and the daunting prospect of prying them open flayed him raw on the inside?

He'd forged a new life for himself. He'd overcome impossible odds to position himself as a formidable adversary but also a considerate ruler in record time.

Wasn't it worth it to reverse this distance his own fears and insecurities had created? Even if for the sake of his unborn child?

No. Not just for his child.

For the woman who dominated his thoughts and fired up his emotions to such a degree, Javid was certain he'd passed the point where he could dismiss her importance or vitality to him. The woman who'd taken to her role as Queen with such grace and equanimity that the Riyaali people had fallen under her spell in a few short weeks.

He froze in his pacing as that admission shook through him. Staggered him.

Then he gritted his jaw.

They'd found such perfect sync on the island after their challenging start. *Na'am*, the stakes felt much higher now. But wouldn't the reward be worth it if he triumphed?

Steely fire lit through his blood as he crossed the room and threw the doors open. Amin, who had replaced Wilfred, his private secretary, immediately jumped up from his desk, eager and bright-eyed despite the early hour.

'May I assist you with anything, Your Majesty?'

Javid paused, glanced down at himself, and grimaced. 'Reschedule my urgent appointments for this afternoon. Cancel everything else for the day.'

The level-headed man barely blinked at the unusual request. 'Of course, Your Majesty. And will you be reachable this morning?'

Not if everything went according to plan. 'No, I'm having breakfast with my wife, then spending the rest of the day with her—' He stopped and frowned when Amin shifted and cleared his throat. 'What is it?'

'Your wife is not in the palace, Your Majesty. She left an hour ago to visit the proposed site for the Expo. She'll be gone all day.'

Javid suppressed a curse and dragged his fingers through his hair. The urge to go after her was immediate and urgent, but, after their strained interaction recently, would she welcome him interrupting her day? Besides, for what he'd planned, he required privacy. Because he wouldn't be averse to ending their tumult by getting very naked with his beautiful wife.

'Forget my instructions, then,' he bit out, his every sense mired in frustration. 'But let me know as soon as she returns.'

'Of course, Your Majesty.'

CHAPTER NINE

THE SITE FOR the future Expo was everything Anaïs could've wished for. And when the combined team of architects, planners and tourism advisors concurred that the venue was now number one on the shortlist, she tried to summon the same excitement she'd felt when she'd discussed the event with Javid.

Everything seemed to throw her back to the idyllic days of her honeymoon. Which in turned squeezed her heart and made her inexplicably teary.

The tears she'd stubbornly attributed to pregnancy hormones.

The heartbreak however...

She mustered a smile when Faiza approached. 'Do you wish to accompany the smaller group to the lake they propose to use for the marine exhibits?'

After being cooped up in the palace for the two-day sandstorm, she didn't relish returning there, especially with Javid's marked absence reinforcing the fact that her new state didn't shift his indifference one iota.

Besides, she'd discovered early on in her PR career that being meticulous avoided confusion and missteps. 'I'll go to the lake. But you can return to the palace. It's been a long day for you.' When Faiza started to shake her head, Anaïs smiled. 'I insist. Because the sandstorm lasted longer than anticipated, my schedule is going to be crazy for the next few days. I need you to go back and start managing expectations for me.'

A clearly reluctant Faiza stared back at her. 'If you're sure? I can do that from here—'

'I'm sure,' she insisted gently. Her assigned bodyguards kept a discreet distance, whereas Faiza was always close by, a situation requiring Anaïs to constantly maintain her composure. She craved an hour or two of not being under her aide's sharp-eyed scrutiny. 'I'll be right behind you.'

Faiza remained hesitant, her gaze probing Anaïs's. Anaïs hadn't shared the news of the pregnancy with her, but the other woman's expression made her wonder if her secret was evident for all to see. 'Your Majesty—'

'I'm fine, Faiza. Go.' She cringed at the sliver of desperation in her voice.

Thankfully, Faiza got the message. With a nod and curtsy, she departed with two bodyguards, leaving Anaïs with a smaller group.

With half of her six-vehicle motorcade, they

headed north. Anaïs had stopped checking her phone for messages hours ago when she realised the mobile service was sketchy this far north— not that Javid would contact her.

In the cool interior of her SUV, with nothing but her thoughts for company, she couldn't escape the glaring evidence of her emotions any longer.

She'd done the unthinkable and fallen in love with Javid Al-Riyaal.

Probably had that morning on the terrace in Bora Bora when she'd needed very little convincing to give her body to her husband. Only she hadn't just given her body. She'd given her heart and her soul. Her mind, body and future. In hope that they could forge a partnership in bed and out of it for the betterment of Riyaal and its people, and for each other.

He'd shown her that the role she'd been reluctant to accept could be the very thing she'd been born for. And she'd finally embraced it, believing he'd be at her side for it.

Now that future stretched before her, inescapable and desolate. Because how could she walk away when she was the mother of the next heir to the throne? How could she—?

She gasped as tyres screeched on the dirt road. A sickening crunch sounded behind her and she spun around to see the vehicle following lying on its side. Her own vehicle tilted precariously, smashing her shoulder against the door, before swerving to a halt.

Shouts of warning rang out. Seconds later, a face appeared in the window, the head of the individual wrapped entirely in a hood. Cold, merciless eyes studied her, then gestured for her to open the door.

'No!' her security chief countermanded tersely. 'Whatever happens, stay in the vehicle, Your Majesty.'

Anaïs went to nod, then froze when acrid smoke started to fill the interior. She had a split second to grasp what was happening before fear clawed up her throat. 'I can't. The smoke. I can't breathe it in! My…my…' *baby!* She wasn't sure whether she screamed the word or merely thought it.

Her hand went to the door handle.

'Your Majesty!' Her bodyguard dived for her hand, staying it before she could open the door.

She whipped around to face him. 'They're going to get in one way or another. This way we have a chance.'

He stared at her grimly, helpless resolution in his eyes. 'We'll stay with you. Do not allow yourself to be separated from us.'

Despite his words, Anaïs knew the moment she opened the door, the situation would be out of their hands.

Her vision was starting to blur.

Terrified of breathing in more fumes, she wrenched again at the door handle.

Anaïs's last, fervent prayer as she slid into unconsciousness was that the baby she already loved more than life itself wouldn't be harmed.

It came as no surprise to Javid that his concentration was shot to pieces all day long. No amount of regal entitlement could disguise his staff's irritation by his incessant demands whether his wife was back.

Amin had taken to voluntarily updating him that 'No, Her Majesty hasn't returned yet' every ten minutes.

So when his private secretary knocked and entered, he was already sighing his disappointment as he looked up. To see the stricken look on Amin's face.

He jerked upright. 'What is it?'

'Your Majesty, there's been report of an attack on Her Majesty's motorcade.'

His vision turned white-hot with terror even as cold dread swelled in his veins. 'Where?'

Amin waved at the flashing phone on Javid's desk. 'One of her security detail managed to call the guards bringing back Her Majesty's private secretary before the line went dead. Faiza is on the line and your head of security is on his way here.'

Javid sucked in a long breath that shook pathetically. Then he snatched up the phone. 'Explain to me why you're not with my wife,' he breathed as soon as the halting voice responded.

'I'm so sorry, Your Majesty, but she insisted I return to the palace.'

'Why?'

'I… I think she wanted…she wanted a little time to herself.'

'Again, why?' Javid growled, his heart thrashing hard enough to hurt his ribs. 'Tell me everything that went on from the moment you left the palace this morning.'

The woman recited Anaïs's itinerary without faltering and with each task his wife had undertaken, Javid was alternately proud and furious.

She was pregnant with his child, for heaven's sake. And yet she'd put in enough work to fell three grown men. As much as he wanted to flay the woman at the end of the phone for deserting Anaïs, and for splitting her security detail—because no senior member of the royal staff was allowed to leave the palace without a full retinue of security, and he knew Anaïs wouldn't have left Faiza without protection—he attempted to retain some rationality.

When it was clear Faiza had nothing else to offer but abject apologies, Javid ended the call, just as his security chief, a tall, muscled man in pristinely pressed khakis, entered. His regimented manner didn't hide the fretful look in his eyes.

'What do we know of my wife's whereabouts?' Javid snapped, uncaring that his voice was an unforgiving blade, intent on drawing retribution on whosoever meant his family harm.

'One of my men managed a five-second call before the line died. The attackers disabled two of the three vehicles. Her Majesty's was intact but...' He paused, gritted his teeth. 'But they used a smoke device to get them to open the doors. Every indication is that they took her. Only her,' he finished gravely.

Javid staggered backwards, his vision blurring as pure terror took hold of him. He swallowed hard. Twice. 'Do we know who they are? Where they took her?'

'Not yet. It happened less than fifteen minutes ago.'

Javid shook himself free of the debilitating fear, bunching his fists as he marched towards the door. 'Was anyone hurt?'

'The guards and the research team she was travelling with were all rendered unconscious but have since woken up. Apart from a few scrapes and bruises when the vehicles were ambushed, they're unharmed.'

Javid clenched his gut against the horror-charged shudder sweeping through him. 'I'm assuming you have a location?'

'Yes, sire. But—'

'Take me there. Now.'

The helicopter ride was the longest of his life, every mile of it spent in a blistering loop of self-castigation, guilt, and pleading with every deity in existence for his wife's safety. When worst-case scenarios played gleefully across his brain, he gritted his teeth and forced himself to breathe.

He would get her back. Whole and unharmed. No other outcome would suffice. And then he would plead some more. Because this half-life he'd fooled himself into believing was enough was lamentably worthless without her.

He would get her back.

The words pounded through his brain as he alighted from the chopper and stalked to the open passenger door of the vehicle his wife had been forced to vacate. The sight of her discarded bag, its contents strewn across the seat and floor, ejected an unholy sound from his throat. He snatched up her mobile phone, gripping it in a vain effort to connect with her.

Absurdly, it offered a moment's clarity, enough for him to spin around to face his security chief. 'Are the drones in place?' he barked.

'Yes, sire. The ground trackers have also been dispatched. We will find her, Your Majesty.'

Javid's grip tightened until he felt the plastic crack. And for as long as he lived, he feared he would associate it with the sound of his own soul cracking with despair. '*Na'am.* But when?'

The older man paled at the raw words and what-ever he saw on Javid's face.

Wisely accepting that there was no prudent response, he discreetly absented himself, leaving his king to nightmare thoughts he wouldn't wish on his worst enemy.

Anaïs came to in slow increments.

First the rustle of what sounded like an animal scurrying about.

Then came the discomfort in her shoulder, probably stemming from the hard surface she lay on.

The pounding headache soon took precedence over everything else once it registered.

She blinked her eyes open, startled at the sight of the cute dog watching her with curious eyes before barking and scampering away.

Then, at the rush of memory, she gasped, her hand immediately darting to her belly. Heart pounding with alarm, she struggled to sit up just as a stylishly dressed woman about her age entered, followed by an older man whose flinty eyes narrowed on her, his expression closed but not malevolent.

Anaïs told herself to cling to that sliver of hope, but still her heart raced, her palms growing clammy. The woman silently poured a glass of water and held it out to her. Unwilling to risk causing offence, she took it but didn't drink despite her deep thirst.

'Do you know who I am?' the man asked.

Anaïs gave a small nod. 'You're Hamid Al-Mejdi's oldest son.'

'*Na'am,*' he confirmed, then said nothing else.

'Where am I?' Anaïs croaked, swallowing when the effort to speak hurt her throat.

The man shrugged. 'Don't worry yourself about location, Your Majesty. It's neither here nor there.'

She sat up straighter as memories unfolded further. The crash. The smoke. *Her team.* 'The people I was with. Where are they? What have you done with them?' She felt momentary relief that she'd sent Faiza back early.

'We have no use for them. We left them behind. They're unharmed.'

Anaïs took courage from the fact that he was answering questions, not making her suffer in silence. 'Then what do you want with me?'

'From you, we want nothing. Your husband, however...'

The unspoken words achieved their aim of triggering panic.

She stared longingly at the water, before lifting her head, fixing him with a bold stare. 'How long have I been here?'

The question finally garnered the barest hint of a smile. 'Long enough to focus His Majesty's mind, we hope.'

Anger reared up, made her head throb harder, but Anaïs didn't care in that moment. 'If you're using me to blackmail him, it's not going to work.'

'Then why has he been searching under every rock in a hundred-mile radius for you?'

Anaïs opened her mouth, then prudently kept her silence. Telling this stranger that her husband was possessive about things he deemed his might not be productive. Instead, she glanced at her surroundings.

The room she was in was windowless. Perhaps a storage room. A deliberate manoeuvre to keep her in the literal dark, she suspected. 'How long do you plan to hold me?'

Again he smiled. 'Long enough to ensure my concerns are heeded. But not long enough to harm you. Or the child you carry.'

Anaïs gasped, the hand gripping the glass shaking. 'H-how did you know?'

'My wife has given me four healthy children. I know the signs. And you just confirmed it.'

She swallowed a moan of despair. 'Javid...the King won't be happy about this. You should let me go.'

He turned towards the door, speaking over his shoulder. 'In good time. Drink the water. I assure you we don't mean you any harm. Food will be brought to you shortly. And when I return, I may or may not enlighten you about the King you think so highly of.'

Only the intervals of the meals that followed gave her an inkling of the passage of time. Or she was completely off track, and they were feeding her dinner for breakfast in a bid to confuse her? Four meals later, she suspected she'd been held a day and a half. Maybe a little more.

Time played havoc with her imagination. Especially after the bombshell her captor had dropped in her lap during her third meal.

The one that confirmed that everything Javid had told her had been a lie.

She jumped to her feet when her captor entered, the young woman close behind. Another tray of food and drink was placed on the bedside table next to her makeshift bed. But they didn't leave immediately.

He pulled what looked like a satellite phone from his pocket and pressed a button. In the silence of the room the dial tone echoed once before it was answered.

'Your Majesty, I think you've been awaiting my call. It's good to hear you've come to an agreement with my father,' her captor said.

'Your father, yes. But not you. You sealed your fate by taking what's mine, Al-Mejdi. Harm a single hair on my wife's head and you will feel the consequences for generations to come,' Javid warned in a voice so sinister, it sent shivers down her spine.

Before Al-Mejdi could respond, the line went dead.

That was when she heard the sound of the helicopter rotor above that of a hundred rumbling engines.

Her husband had arrived. And he'd brought a veritable army with him. Her panicked captor raced outside, and Anaïs heard the sound of raised voices, followed by urgent pleas.

The door was flung back on its hinges and Javid filled the doorway, his riveting form clad from head to toe in black. He strode across the room, every inch the merciless marauder.

Relief, gratitude and a surge of hormones made her sag back down onto the bed. He rushed forward but then stopped.

For an age, he just stared down at her, his features ashen and pinched, the only movement the flare of his nostrils as he breathed.

Then, bending low, he scooped her up, cradling her against his massive chest as if she were an infant. Anaïs found that she didn't want to protest. That, just for this moment, she would bask in his heat and strength.

Terror of the unknown and fears for the safety of her baby had worn her out. So she tucked her head against his chest, and let his steady heartbeat calm her own.

For some reason, that motion seemed to trigger something untamed in Javid. His arms tightened a fraction harder as he spun on his heel and walked them both into the sunlight. Squeezing her eyes against the harsh glare, she curled her hand over his nape.

'Arrest them,' he snarled to somebody. 'Every single one. I will deal with them later.'

Two hours later, Anaïs was back in the palace, bathed and tucked into the warmth of her bed.

The doctor had performed a thorough exam under Javid's watchful eye and prescribed a few days' bed rest and lots of fluids.

She clutched her box of tissues close. It seemed the roller coaster of emotions had left her with an overflow of tears. But as much as she didn't want to exhibit further weakness in front of Javid, her hormones had different ideas.

Now, she watched him pace back and forth across her carpet, occasionally raking his fingers through his hair. She'd discovered from a distraught Faiza that she had been gone for four days.

Javid hadn't shaved during that time, if the stubble gracing his jaw was an indication. That she found it intensely sexy was another poor mark against her hopeless emotion for this man. Even worse when Al-Mejdi had shown her his true colours.

To counteract that sensation, she spoke up, eager to end the torment of having him close and yet so far away. 'Thank you for coming to get me.

I'm not ashamed to admit I was…terrified for a while there.'

He froze, made a sound that curiously resembled a wounded wild animal, but she dismissed it, even while she dashed the tears from her eyes.

'I hope I never have to be in the position to return the favour, but I owe you—'

One hand slashed through the air, his face clouding in a frown. 'Stop talking like that. You owe me nothing! I would pay a million times to keep you safe!'

'What did you have to pay for my release, out of interest?'

He waved her away again. 'It doesn't matter—'

'It matters to me. Tell me,' she insisted, ignoring her shaking voice.

His lips compressed and a muscle ticced at his temple. 'There will be no roles in my government for any Al-Mejdi, of course, but I agreed to the original concessions Adnan promised—reduced tariffs on their imported goods in return for helping my cousin broker peace in the northern region. What Adnan failed to see was that they created the very situation they claimed to have helped solve. It was a ploy they've used several times.'

'Then why did you agree to it?'

Astonishment lit his eyes. 'Do you really need to ask me that? Do you know what I went through while you were held captive, Anaïs?' His voice was gruff. Raw.

But she didn't delude herself into thinking she was the cause of it. 'Stop acting as if I'm important to you.' Her hand cradled her belly. 'As if *we* are important!'

'What was the alternative? That I calmly sit at the negotiating table and bargain with your life? Or would you have preferred me to leave you there and toss about excuses as to your whereabouts while I went about my day?'

'At least we're getting somewhere,' she retorted bitterly.

He dragged harsh fingers through his hair, his eyebrows clamped in a frown. 'What are you talking about?'

She sucked in a breath and held it for the longest time before exhaling. But it still didn't curb the anguish she knew she would feel if he indicated there was truth in her next question.

'Did you make an agreement with the royal council that you would only rule Riyaal for ten years? That after that you didn't care who they found to rule in your place, as long as it wasn't you?' she demanded.

He went rigid with shock, his jaw sagging. But she didn't need to hear him confirm it. She saw her answer in the depths of his eyes.

'Anaïs—'

'Spare me your explanations. Everything is out in the open now, my hypocritical king.'

He inhaled sharply. 'Watch your tongue, *habibti*,' he warned with deadly softness.

'The way you watched yours when you held my feet to the fire about duty and responsibility when you intended to turn your back on yours all along?'

He took one long stride towards her, then almost immediately pivoted to pace away. 'This…a lot has changed since then.' He shook his head. 'You need to rest. This isn't the time to discuss this.'

'You're right. This isn't the time. But you can rest assured we won't need to revisit the subject. *J'en ai fini avec toi.*' She didn't shout or snap the last words. They came from a churning knot of anguish but emerged as calm as a millpond.

Perhaps her soul knew to keep the strength for later, when she would need to draw on her reserves.

Javid looked thunderstruck. And she realised that speaking the words in French had finally got through to him. His game of cards had come tumbling down. Still, because he was who he was, he took a determined step towards her, his eyes narrowing in rejection of her statement.

Anaïs turned away from him, pulled the sheets up to her chin and fixed her gaze on the wall.

Tense minutes passed.

Then he left the room, taking every ounce of

vitality with him, along with the composure she'd exercised to keep her heartache in check.

Deprived of it, she finally sagged into the sheets, and let the sobs rip free.

For the next three months, they maintained a civil front. When the official announcement was made about her pregnancy, she smiled for well-wishing staff and the doting subjects when she was out in public.

Her due date was decreed a holiday in Riyaal and the kingdom finally shook itself free from the tragedy of losing its previous king and queen, in anticipation of the hopeful news.

In public, Anaïs and Javid were the ultimate modern royal couple. They held hands. They cheered on their favourite teams at sports events and hosted public ceremonies as a unit. On rare occasions when she forgot herself—or perhaps when the agony of unrequited love grew too much to bear—she even allowed Javid to drift a hand over the small bump where their baby grew.

But what the public didn't know was that they attended every event together because Javid refused to let her out of his sight when they weren't behind the safety of palace walls.

Discreetly, her kidnappers had been charged, had their day in court and been found guilty. They were no longer a threat.

To all intents and purposes, things could return to normal.

Except they couldn't. The yawning gulf between her and Javid had grown insurmountable. Enough for Anaïs to contemplate retreat for the sake of her heart and her sanity.

And when Javid appeared in her suite the next morning for their first ultrasound, she knew she couldn't take it any more.

She barely managed to hold it together as he took her hand and led her to the special bed set up in the living room.

'Are you ready, Your Majesties?' the doctor asked with a smile.

Anaïs looked up, not at the doctor but at her husband, to find his eyes fixed on her. The morning sickness had passed and, at just under five months, the swell of her belly was visible when she wore certain styles.

This morning, she wore peach-coloured trousers and a matching top made of soft, thin jersey wool. With her hair brushed out and minimal make-up, she felt a little self-conscious, especially with that single-minded gaze Javid was focusing on her.

When he reached for her hand, she knew it was only for show.

And yet, she couldn't stop her fingers from curling around his, his warmth making her yearning intensify.

'We're ready,' Javid said.

'Would you like to know the gender?'

Again her gaze darted to Javid's. He raised an eyebrow and she exhaled. *'Oui.'*

'Na'am,' he echoed.

'Your daughter looks absolutely perfect and healthy,' the doctor said.

They glanced at the screen and her heart lurched.

It should've been the best moment of their lives.

Anaïs concentrated on the doctor's words only because she didn't want to miss anything important. But her heart screamed in agony throughout.

The moment the doctor left, she pulled her hand from Javid's and placed much-needed space between them.

'Last week, the doctor said a change of scene would be beneficial, preferably by the sea. I'm thinking of spending some time at the Emerald Palace.'

It was a white lie. Her doctor had advocated fresh air, which she could find by walking in the palace's extensive gardens, not at an entirely different location.

The Emerald Palace, so named for the dazzling jewel-coloured waters that lapped at its craggy shores to the west and its pristine beach to the south, was the perfect choice. The pictures she'd seen of it were breathtaking. Faiza had assured her reality was even better.

Javid nodded. 'I can arrange for us to spend some time there. I'll need a few days to get some time-sensitive duties out of the way.'

'I…what? You're not coming with me, are you?'

His eyes narrowed. 'You weren't thinking I'd let you go alone, were you?'

'I…yes, I was thinking exactly that, as it happens.'

His nostrils flared. 'That's out of the question.'

'No, it's not. And before you cite safety, you've tripled my security since the incident. I couldn't be more secure if I was tucked inside Fort Knox!'

'Be that as it may, I will—'

'Javid, I don't want you there!'

He froze, his every feature hardening. Then his eyes grew bleak. 'You have it all worked out, haven't you? This campaign to exclude me?'

She didn't miss the swell of bitterness in his voice. And it only exacerbated her own. 'If you didn't want this, then you shouldn't have misled me.'

He opened his mouth, and she found herself yearning for a fight. For something that would prove any of this bothered him beyond the aesthetics of the situation.

But, as he'd become prone to doing, Javid merely spun on his heel and left.

And on legs that felt shaky with despair, she summoned Faiza and gave instructions for her belongings to be packed.

CHAPTER TEN

HE WAS OFFICIALLY at his wits' end.

More than that, he was conclusively terrified he was losing Anaïs. For one long, excruciating month, he'd respected her wishes and stayed away.

Sure, she returned to the palace often enough to sustain the public impression that things were perfect between them. But she could never wait to get away.

And he'd had enough of it.

So he felt a smug kind of satisfaction when he screeched his sports car to a halt outside the double doors of the Emerald Palace and saw her shocked face behind the butler's in the hallway.

'Javid. What are you doing here?'

Some said his arrogance was innate, a thing he'd been born with. He could've reached for it, reminded her that he was a prince turned King. That everything his gaze rested on, including the damn horizon, belonged to him and therefore he had every right to be here.

But that was the old Javid. He was attempting to be different.

Still…not *too* different. Because there was something within him that had made her smile once upon a time. Made her spew a torrent of French when her emotions were deliciously high and unfettered.

He pocketed the keys and vaulted up the steps to where his wife stood. Nodded a dismissal at the staff once the bowing and scraping was over and his bodyguards had assured themselves that he was safely indoors and absented themselves. When they reached the living room, he pinned her with his gaze.

'I've allowed this state of play to go on too long.'

One perfectly shaped eyebrow slanted at him. 'Have you? Or are you merely escaping your mother's presence?'

For a scant moment, he fooled himself into thinking she was teasing him. But nothing on her beautiful face indicated humour. While she glowed from head to toe, her eyes were dull, the sparkle and spirit he'd revelled in during their honeymoon dimmed.

He'd discovered that there wasn't much he wouldn't do to win that spark back, including finally giving in to Tahir's grumbling request to meet with his mother—most likely to get their mother off *his* back.

The result of his agreement had been strained dinners two evenings in a row and the conclusion that he didn't want a repeat performance. Unless he had back-up in the form of his wife.

'She's asking to meet you. Apparently, she didn't get the chance at our wedding, and she feels slighted.'

'Is that why you're here? To summon me back for another performance?'

'Would that make you more amenable to my presence?'

She sighed. 'Javid—'

'No,' he growled, sensing what was coming. Then he exerted his willpower over his panic. Over the real and present fear that he was running out of time. 'Don't send me away. Not again.' The naked plea in his voice didn't perturb him. He would crawl through volcanoes for this woman.

'You're the King, as you've mentioned once or twice in the past. I can't send you anywhere. I don't have that power.'

Dark laughter scraped his throat. '*Na'am*, you have all the power. And it terrifies me that you choose not to use it because you don't think it's worth it. That *I'm* worth it.'

'I...what are you talking about?'

'You can't stand me. That's why you left our bed. That's why you hide out here, isn't it?'

Her laughter sounded like a feminine echo of his. '*T'es sérieux?*' she snapped, incredulous.

The deep longing that punched him in the gut evidenced how much he'd missed hearing her speak her father tongue. How much he wanted more of it. 'Yes, I'm serious. If it's not true, tell me why you've left me.'

'I'm here because you pushed me away! Because you turned cold the moment we boarded the plane to come home!' She shook her head, her luscious hair rippling about her shoulders. Then she went one better and flung her hands in the air. '*Comment oses-tu?* How dare you turn this around on me? You left me long before I left you!'

He swallowed, all his fears congealing in his gut. He was too late.

'But then you never intended to stick around, did you? Ten years, wasn't it? Long enough to show everyone what a brilliant ruler you could be before you left? That's how things work with you, isn't it? You make yourself irreplaceable, then walk away, leaving everyone needing you. *C'est ton modus operandi.*'

It was his turn to be incredulous. To dredge through painful memories. 'Irreplaceable? I'm the one thing everyone wants a piece of until I outlive my usefulness. I was never meant to be King. Never meant to be the one that anyone wanted. For as long as I can remember, I've just been a useful ornament, Anaïs. Perhaps a fixer, at best. But you, you're the real deal. Did I bargain to rule Riyaal for a fixed time? Yes, I did. But only because I believed there was someone better for the role. Someone like you, *habibti*.'

Her eyes had been widening as he spoke. Now her mouth gaped too. 'Someone better? Me? *T'es sérieux?*' she demanded again.

Javid conjured up a smile. 'I insisted you stay because I knew, once you got over how all this came around, that you would have the whole of Riyaal falling in love with you. And they have.'

'But… I didn't want the throne. I don't want to rule. Not if it's without…' She stopped, shook her head. 'We're getting away from the point.'

'That I left you before you left me? *Na'am*, I did. Because I was terrified that I would be put on the shelf once more. That I would outlive my usefulness or scare you away with how much I wanted you.'

'How…why?'

He pressed his lips together, the seemingly inevitable exhumation of the past weighing on him. 'My father couldn't have made it plainer that I was surplus to requirements if he tried. My reaction to that was to…act out when I was younger. Then, when I was older, it was to leave Jukrat and live a certain lifestyle that I knew would get under his skin.'

'And I'm assuming it did?' she asked.

'Oh, yes. But even then, I wanted to counter that in a way that made him realise I wasn't completely useless. So I excelled in diplomacy, a skill needed with his council and he couldn't dismiss in his son. The first time he requested my services, I wanted to gloat like no one had gloated before.'

Did he catch the faintest twitch of her beautiful lips?

He forced himself to continue, to dig deeper into the bitter well that had been his childhood. 'I didn't, by the way. I was too busy being thankful that he needed me. That I was useful to him. But the moment he was done with me, he went back to pretending I didn't exist. That has been the cycle of my life.'

'But I never used you. I never treated you like that,' she whispered, her voice a knot of bruised hurt. 'On the island, you made me believe we were equals, that you valued me. But then you froze me out, except in bed. I thought I was just a body to you, not a woman with a mind and feelings.'

His chest tightened and for a moment he feared he was having a heart attack. 'You weren't and we were...*are* equals. But I'd never had anything like that, you see. And it terrified me how much I wanted it. I used the excuse of the challenges of ruling to distance myself because I feared rejection was coming.'

'But it didn't. I never rejected you.'

'Sometimes the fear of the trauma is greater than the trauma itself. I'd been conditioned that way and I didn't know a way out of it.'

She wrapped her arms around her middle,

throwing her swelling belly into relief. Need poured through him, and it wasn't even the sexual kind. It was the heart and soul kind, the kind that made him want to kneel at her feet and worship her for the rest of his days.

'But I'm changing, *mon soleil.*'

She shook her head, her expression still locked in hurt and sorrow. 'You were able to turn off your feelings so easily. It was terrifying.'

'No. I never turned them off. I only learned to disguise them. But I can't keep doing it, Anaïs. Not any more. These past months have been hell. I've lived in a cycle of regret and terror that I've ruined everything. That not taking the chance to tell you how I felt that morning before you left for the Expo site will be my one greatest mistake for ever.'

She frowned. '*Arrêt*…you were coming to find me that morning?'

'I'd spent three days regretting how I reacted when you told me I was going to be a father—another thing that I believed I was nowhere near qualified for, by the way—but I kept thinking how in sync we were on the island. And yes, I also needed to tell you how sorry I was for my behaviour. Discovering you were gone, that you'd been captured…'

She swayed forward and, absolutely gambling his last card, he caught her. When she didn't flinch away or demand he let her go, he pushed his luck further and wrapped one arm around her waist.

'Those four days were the worst of my life, *mon soleil.*'

'For both of us,' she whispered. 'I didn't know whether I'd ever see you again.'

A sound ejected from his throat, a hoarse mess that echoed the sensation inside. 'I failed in my duty to protect you. For that, I'll always regret it.'

Her hand fluttered, then rose to cup his jaw. 'It wasn't your fault. The fault lies with the people who took me. Never you.'

Javid wanted to shout his joy to the heavens at her touch. But he wasn't done. He needed to revisit this once, then put it behind him. Behind *them*.

'What would you have said if you'd found me that morning?' she prompted, her voice hesitant. A hesitation he'd put there with his actions.

'I would've begged your forgiveness for letting my past get in the way of my present,' he offered immediately. Then he laid one hand on the firm curve of her stomach, where his daughter grew. 'In the way of our future.'

A shudder went through her, and tears filmed her eyes. 'Don't cry, *habibti*. These beautiful eyes should never shed tears, ever again.'

'*Les hormones.* And tears of happiness.'

He brushed them away with his thumbs, hope growing in his heart. 'I would also have told you that I loved you. That the prospect of living without you had terrified me more than what my past trauma had led me to expect. That I would do anything for another chance to build on what we started on the island.'

The hand on his jaw shook as it curved over his nape. As she drew closer until they shared one breath. 'Do you know what I would've said?'

'Tell me,' he mock growled, his voice thick with every emotion he'd futilely tried to suppress.

'I would've told you that I loved you too. That I want nothing more than to be your wife. To build a family with you and rule by your side. Not in your stead, because you're insanely talented at being King, *mon coeur*. The people of Riyaal have exactly who they need and desire on the throne.'

'Call me that again,' he begged gruffly.

Her smile widened. *'Mon coeur.'*

He groaned, then dropped his head to *finally* kiss his wife. When they separated long minutes later, her eyes were shining bright. And he swore then and there that he would never be the cause of them growing dull again.

Her thumb moved over his lips, and he pressed a kiss to it.

'I love you, Javid. I can't wait for our lives to start properly. I can't wait for our little one to be here.' She laughed. 'And I can't wait to properly meet your mother.'

His groan this time was a little pained. 'There's much work to be done there.'

'I know. But you relish challenges, *mon beau roi*. I know you'll excel at this one too.'

He kissed her again, long and deep, because he'd found the missing piece of his soul. And when he raised his head, the depth of his happiness staggered him. 'I'll put in the work on one condition.'

'Name it.'

'That everything you just said about loving me and starting our lives?'

'Oui?'

'Say it all again. But in French.'

'Avec plaisir, mon amour.'

EPILOGUE

Five years later

JAVID APPROACHED HIS brother where he stood on the deck of his yacht, drink in hand as he observed the impressive display before him. Hearing his footsteps, Tahir turned to him with a droll look.

'If you're about to play "my flotilla is bigger than yours", save your breath.'

Rich laughter barked from him, an act he'd found himself indulging in with dizzying frequency over the past five years. He shrugged inwardly. What could he say? Laughter came easily when one was insanely happy.

'I wasn't planning on it, but now that you mention it…' He laughed some more when Tahir huffed in mock irritation.

Together they watched the passage of brightly decorated sea vessels in all shapes and sizes that formed the denouement of the three-day spectacular Festival of Abundance.

Javid's grandfather had founded the annual

festivities, and, with enthusiastic nudging from Anaïs, he'd incorporated it into Riyaali custom three years ago, much to the delight of their subjects.

In times past Javid had avoided the festival like a plague, finding an excuse to be absent from Jukrat. He'd had no reason to feel thankful for his so-called abundance back then. Not when what truly mattered—love, acceptance—was lacking.

Now...

Female laughter sounded from behind them, and, like iron poles drawn by two mighty magnets, the brothers turned. From the corner of his eye, Javid watched the irritation melt from Tahir's face as his gaze fixed on his pregnant wife. He would've mocked the sappiness on his brother's face if he didn't know his own held the same for his wife.

Whatever joke his sister-in-law, Queen Lauren, was telling the group of female friends and relatives made his own wife howl with laughter, even as Anaïs, gloriously pregnant too, covered the ears of their adorable four-year-old daughter, Djamila.

His daughter wriggled free almost immediately, then gleefully chased after her shrieking male cousin.

'I see your daughter is learning the ropes of torturing the males in her life,' Tahir grumbled good-naturedly. 'It'll be good when your son is born to balance things out.'

'Sons,' he delivered smoothly, keeping his face deliberately neutral.

Tahir stiffened in surprise before his head whipped towards Javid. 'What?'

'My beautiful wife is carrying twins. I would've told you earlier but since we're not playing the "mine is bigger than yours" game...?' He shrugged.

Tahir mock punched him on the arm before pulling him into a man hug. When they separated, he was sure his brother was blinking back emotion. Or perhaps it was his own projecting?

Yes, the doctor's announcement three days ago had been a huge shock. He'd alternated between pure elation and mild terror. His wife and daughter had him so wrapped around their little fingers, he didn't know whether he was coming or going most days. Toss in twin sons...

He wasn't sure his heart could contain all the love he felt for his growing family.

Tahir clapped him on the shoulder one more time. 'I'm proud of you, brother.'

Javid nodded, unable to speak past the rock wedged in his throat. After a minute he managed to clear it. 'I heard a little rumour a month ago.'

Again Tahir stiffened but his face gave nothing away. 'Oh?'

'Yes. Something about the council being advised to double-check a loophole in the law surrounding my wife becoming Queen?'

Tahir shrugged. 'They needed to ensure everything was airtight.' Piercing eyes rested on Javid. 'I know a thing or two about letting the right one get away for far too long, even if things are resolved in the end. I didn't want that for you, brother. You deserved to be happy. We both do.'

'*Shukran,*' Javid gruffly thanked his brother.

Tahir smiled, his gaze returning to linger on his pregnant wife and their son. 'Make me the godfather of all your children and I'll consider it thanks enough.'

'Deal,' Javid offered immediately.

'Deal? You're making deals during a festival?' Anaïs softly admonished as she glided towards him, dressed head to toe in white.

Mon Dieu, but she was beautiful. He was utterly biased, of course, but she truly was a breathtaking vision. And she grew lovelier day by day, year by year.

He slid his arm around her waist, pulled her close and kissed her lips.

'Ew!' Djamila spluttered as she joined them.

They laughed as he scooped his daughter up into his arms. Tahir drew a loving finger over his niece's face before sauntering off to reclaim his own wife.

'You know I never miss an opportunity to make deals,' he answered his wife.

She laughed, her eyes twinkling. 'Oh, yes, I'm very familiar with that particular trait.'

He nodded, unable to tear his gaze from her face. 'But none comes close to the priceless deal I made when you allowed me to love and cherish you,' he murmured.

Her breath grew shaky. *'Arrêt tu vas me faire pleurer,'* she whispered, blinking her beautiful eyes.

He trailed more kisses on her cheek, much to the delight and cheering of a passing boatful of Riyaali subjects, and the disgust of their daughter. 'You can cry all you want, my love, as long as they're happy tears.'

Eyes filled with love and happiness locked on his and his heart leapt with pure joy.

'With you, *mon coeur*, they are. Always.'

* * * * *

If you fell head over heels for
His Pregnant Desert Queen
then you'll be captivated by the
first installment in the
Brothers of the Desert duet
Their Desert Night of Scandal
available now!

And make sure to check out these other
Maya Blake stories!

The Commanding Italian's Challenge
The Greek's Hidden Vows
Reclaimed for His Royal Bed
Bound by Her Rival's Baby
A Vow to Claim His Hidden Son

Available now!